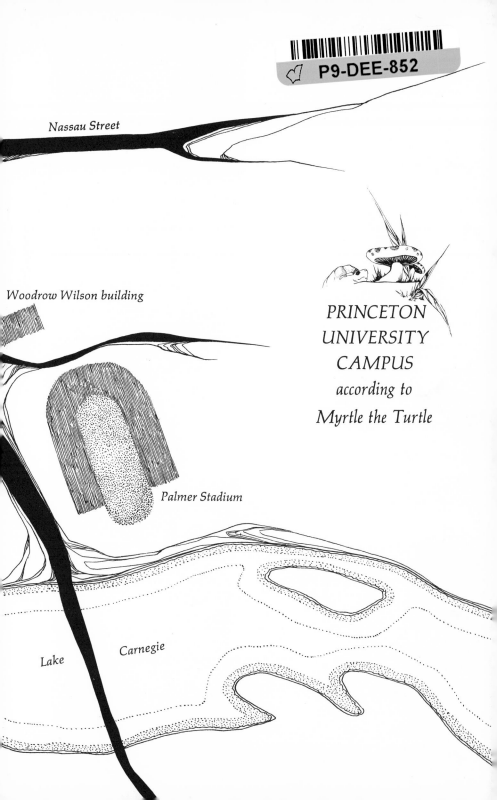

Nassau Street

Woodrow Wilson building

PRINCETON
UNIVERSITY
CAMPUS
according to
Myrtle the Turtle

Palmer Stadium

Lake Carnegie

Tales of Myrtle the Turtle

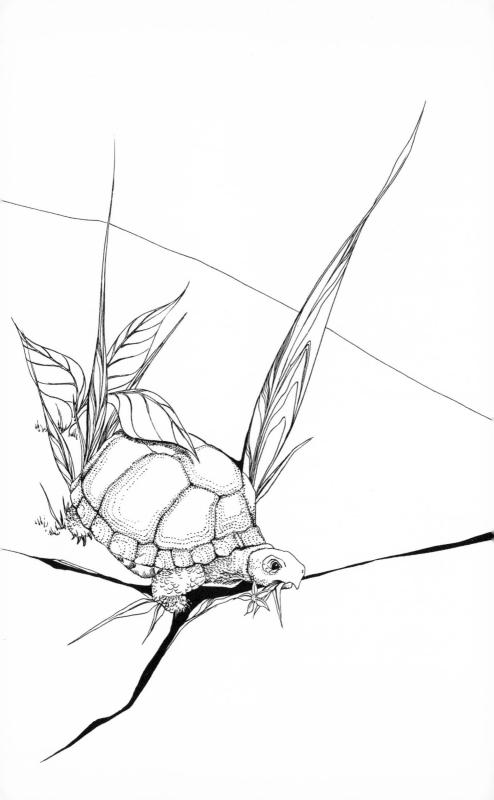

Tales of Myrtle the Turtle

KEITH ROBERTSON

Drawings by Peter Parnall

The Viking Press   New York

First Edition

Copyright © 1974 by Keith Robertson
Illustrations copyright © 1974 by The Viking Press, Inc.
All rights reserved
First published in 1974 by The Viking Press, Inc.
625 Madison Avenue, New York, N.Y. 10022
Published simultaneously in Canada by
The Macmillan Company of Canada Limited
Printed in U.S.A.

1   2   3   4   5   78   77   76   75   74

Library of Congress Cataloging in Publication Data
Robertson, Keith, 1914–   Tales of Myrtle the turtle.
Summary: Adventures of Aunt Myrtle, Uncle Herman, and
other turtles that reside on the Princeton University campus.
[1. Turtles—Fiction]   I. Title. PZ7.R547Tal [Fic] 73–22483

ISBN 0-670-69167-4

Tales of
Myrtle the Turtle

 *one*

My name is Gloria and I am a turtle. As everyone knows, turtles move very slowly. That isn't a handicap at all as some animals like dogs or humans might think. I have a friend, Adolph, who is a dachshund, and they are rather slow for dogs as they have such short legs. He told me that one day a greyhound went by him like a streak. The greyhound was chasing a squirrel and was going so fast that he didn't even see a big juicy hamburger that someone had dropped by mistake. Adolph, who was just waddling along, ate the hamburger. Of course the squirrel went up a tree, and that silly greyhound didn't get anything.

As for people, they race around so fast in automobiles that they have no time to look at anything except other cars and road signs. But we turtles move around very slowly and see all sorts of things. And lots of times we sit in one place for hours and contemplate. My Aunt Myrtle says no other species on earth contemplates as much as we do. Naturally, we have many, many wise thoughts and observations.

Turtles don't write books, but I decided it was time that one did. I tried to persuade Aunt Myrtle to write one, but she said I should. Most of this book will be stories that Aunt Myrtle has told me. She is very, very old and very, very wise. Turtles live almost forever, you know, and Aunt Myrtle is the oldest turtle I've ever met. She isn't exactly my aunt, but maybe my great-great-great-great-great-great-aunt. She says we would have to get a book out of the Princeton University library to find out exactly how many "greats" I should use. The book is called *The Box Turtle Genealogy of America.* I didn't know what a genealogy was, but she explained.

"A genealogy may be defined as a one-sided history of a family," she said, choosing each word carefully as she always does when she explains anything. "It tells you a lot about the rich and famous members of a family and very little about the dumbbells and the crooks."

Since I've never seen this book about my ancestors or family, all I know is that we are box turtles and the five I know are all very nice. The five are my mother, my father, Aunt Myrtle, my kid brother Witherspoon, and me. Witherspoon says dumb things at times, not because he is stupid, but because he is younger than I am and not as well educated. Of course all of the family are much better educated than most turtles because we live on the Princeton University campus. We hear all sorts of lectures, and we can slip into classrooms almost as we want. Aunt Myrtle says Witherspoon and I have much better attendance records than many of the regular students. Aunt Myrtle was around here before Princeton University started, so she has heard about everything five or six times. If she didn't have such a creaky old voice, she could probably give a good lecture on almost any subject taught at Princeton.

Witherspoon and I spend much of our time with Aunt Myrtle. This is particularly true this summer because our parents went to Delaware to visit some of my mother's friends. Aunt Myrtle explains lots of things, and her stories are usually very interesting. Most of them are about her husband Herman. I've never met Herman, but he must have been a wonderful and unusual turtle. He traveled all over the world and did all sorts of exciting things.

"A most exceptional turtle," Aunt Myrtle often says. She sighs every time she mentions Herman. "He had the most unusual eyes. They were pink. Most boy turtles have red eyes like Witherspoon's, just as most girl turtles have yellow eyes like yours, Gloria, or like mine. But Herman's eyes were pink. I remember the first time I looked into those lovely pink eyes of his. 'This is the turtle you've been waiting for,' I said to myself. 'This is your dream turtle.' And I was right. He was much older than I, but that never mattered. We were meant for each other."

"He must have been awful old," Witherspoon said. Witherspoon makes some remarks that aren't very tactful, but as I said, he's young.

"That was long, long ago," Aunt Myrtle said. "I was a mere girl. But as you say, today he would be considered quite old, even for a turtle."

"How old?" Witherspoon insisted.

"We don't keep exact tallies the way people do," Aunt Myrtle said with a sniff. "It's one's attitude about life that is important. But I think he once said he was fourteen years older than Christopher Columbus. He was visiting San Salvador, you know, when Columbus landed there in 1492. We turtles have always known exactly where America is. The people in Europe didn't, so they had to 'discover' it."

Aunt Myrtle knows the Princeton University campus better than anyone because she was here when the first building was built. She has shown Witherspoon and me how to go everywhere. We know all the buildings and all the shortcuts. We know where the juiciest bugs are to be found, and which streets are dangerous to cross. On hot summer nights we go over to the new fountain and pool, outside the Woodrow Wilson building, and go wading. We don't swim much because box turtles aren't crazy about deep water.

Now and then we go over to Nassau Street and watch all the people hurrying in and out of the stores and the policemen hurrying around giving them parking tickets. One day there was a big bus parked next to the curb, taking up two parking spaces. A man and a woman got out just as we arrived and went off down the street. Then a boy got out also and went over to sit on the stone wall, leaving the door open. This didn't look like a regular bus, so Witherspoon and I sneaked over and peeked inside. It was so interesting we went inside and made an inspection tour.

The bus was a complete home on wheels. It had a stove, refrigerator, toilet, shower, table, and several beds.

The air conditioning had been on, and it was cool inside. Witherspoon wanted to stay, but I told him it was foolish. Someone might come back and find us and throw us out on the sidewalk. Even if you have a hard shell to protect you, landing on a sidewalk isn't fun. As we got down from the bottom step and walked back toward the Firestone Library, there was Aunt Myrtle, mad as a hornet. She was tapping her foot on the ground and glaring.

"The minute my back is turned, you two go wandering off and getting into trouble."

"We didn't get into any trouble," I explained.

"And your back wasn't turned when we left," Witherspoon added. "You were faced our way, but your eyes were closed."

"I was not asleep. I was contemplating," Aunt Myrtle said. "That was a foolish act, going inside a motor home that way. Someone might come back and drive off without even seeing you. The next thing you'd know, you'd be in Wyoming, if not in a pot of soup."

Witherspoon and I know that people don't often make soup of box turtles, but neither of us wanted to be carried off to Wyoming. However, Aunt Myrtle always acts much more annoyed than she really is, so we didn't pay much attention to her scolding.

"It was beautiful inside," I said. "Beds, refrigerators, everything."

"They call those motor homes," Aunt Myrtle said. "They're the latest thing with people. Of course they are about a million years or so behind us turtles."

"What do you mean?" I asked.

"Well, turtles invented the same thing, only much better, at the beginning of the glacial period."

"Which glacier?" Witherspoon asked. He was showing off, because I was outside the same window and heard the same geology lecture that he did.

"I really couldn't say," Aunt Myrtle answered, giving Witherspoon an icy look. "Glaciers come and glaciers go. We turtles keep right on regardless."

"Tell us about the invention, please," I said.

"Well, I might be persuaded, but mainly for your sake, Gloria," Aunt Myrtle said. "If we could find a shady spot."

"Persuaded my eye," Witherspoon said to me as we followed Aunt Myrtle. "You couldn't stop her from telling the story." My little brother doesn't have the proper respect for his elders at times.

"Well, a long, long time ago, during the Mesozoic era, we turtles had no shells," Aunt Myrtle began.

"When was this messy zoic era?" Witherspoon asked. "Was that before girls were students at Princeton?"

"Oh much. Much before Princeton. It was millions of years ago when the world was cluttered up with those big clumsy dinosaurs. Man wasn't even around then. After all, man is a latecomer. It's amazing how important he thinks he is when he's been around such a short time. But anyhow, as I said, we turtles had no shells. We had lovely fair skins, and having no heavy shells to carry around, we moved much faster. Most of the world was covered either with water or with marshes filled with beautiful, beautiful mud. There were millions and millions of insects. Turtles could loll around in the nice warm mud and reach out when they were hungry and snap up some of the insects that flew by. Of course nothing is ever perfect, and now and then one of those big awkward brontosauruses would come clomping along and step on a poor turtle and squash him."

"What's a brontosaurus?" I asked.

"A big dinosaur," Aunt Myrtle explained. "They were as big as those trailer trucks that go rumbling down Stockton Street. There were all sorts of dinosaurs —two-footed ones, duck-billed ones, armor-plated ones, and one with three horns on its head. All of them were stupid, but we turtles had to keep well out of their way. Most of them were vegetarians, but some weren't. And any of them could mash you as flat as a big truck can today.

"To get on with my story, the world began to change. It didn't rain so much, and there weren't such huge forests of ferns and trees. The sun shone more, and some of the mud dried. There began to be ice in the north; the days got warmer and the nights got colder. Those silly dinosaurs just couldn't keep up with the changes, and they became extinct."

"What's that mean?" Witherspoon interrupted. "Do you mean they smelled?"

"I mean they all died," Aunt Myrtle said. "I suppose after they had been dead awhile they smelled. Please don't interrupt so much. I'll lose the thread of my story. After all this story was told by Herman's grandmother years ago. She got it from her grandmother, who heard it from her grandmother, and so on."

"There are a lot of grandmothers in Herman's family, aren't there?" Witherspoon asked.

"Just a normal amount," Aunt Myrtle said shortly. "All of us are descended from a long line of ancestors. Now where was I, Gloria?"

"The world was changing," I reminded her.

"Oh yes. And we turtles had no shells. I wasn't alive then, but I suppose we were similar in a way to those lizards one sees in the south. Anyhow, life became very difficult. Our fair skins were very delicate from having soaked ourselves in that lovely oozy mud. When we went out in the sun for long, we got sunburned. When the sun was under a cloud, or at night, it was frequently cold. Hundreds and thousands of turtles got the sniffles, something that never happened when we could soak in that lovely mud. The health of the whole turtle population was threatened. So a huge conference was called. You understand that there were a number of different kinds of families of turtles by then. Some big, some small, some who spent most of their time in the water, and some who spent most of their time on land like us.

"Well, a number of ideas were suggested. The turtles who liked the water felt that we should live in the water and weave clothes out of seaweed if we got cold. Another thought we should stay on land and carry mushroom parasols. There were lots of mushrooms everywhere in those days, and you could pick almost any size you wanted. This wasn't a bad idea as far as the sun was concerned, but a mushroom wasn't much help in keeping you warm on the cold days. I suppose you could eat it if it wasn't too dried out. Mushrooms are very nutritious, I've heard."

"What does nutritious mean?" Witherspoon asked. I didn't know either, but I've learned that if I keep quiet and look very superior when there's a word I don't know, Witherspoon will usually ask.

"That means full of food value," Aunt Myrtle said. "But for food to keep you warm, there's nothing like a good fat grub." She stretched out her neck and caught a nice white grub that was climbing up the stem of a plant. It looked delicious.

"To get back to this meeting, some people thought we ought to burrow deep in the ground and live there most of the time the way the moles have done. Others suggested we try to build houses out of bark. A few of them did. They talked and talked and got nothing decided just like humans when they have a conference. You've listened to enough of them right here at Princeton to know what I mean. The problem was finally solved by a turtle who had been sort of an outcast. He was an ancestor of your uncle Herman. He was called Old Smooth and Ugly Herman."

"That's a silly name," Witherspoon said. "Why didn't he have an ordinary name like Witherspoon?"

"Because there were no streets in New Jersey to name him after," Aunt Myrtle said. "And besides he was smooth and he was ugly. As far back as turtle history goes, and that is practically forever, wrinkles have always been a sign of great beauty. Take me for instance."

Aunt Myrtle has a very wrinkled and aristocratic-looking neck. Even Witherspoon admits that the folds of fat around her neck are lovely.

"Most creatures in the world, except humans, admire wrinkles," Aunt Myrtle continued. "I understand people take mud baths of get rid of wrinkles. Any turtle knows that mud baths cause wrinkles. I don't know why Old Smooth and Ugly was so smooth, but he hadn't a wrinkle on his body except one or two around his ankles. I understand that he was an exceptionally ugly turtle, and all the other turtles laughed at him. So he spent most of the time off by himself. It happened that he liked a spot beside a rock under a big conifer tree." Aunt Myrtle saw the look in Witherspoon's eye, so she explained before he could ask. "Most evergreens are conifers. This particular kind disappeared thousands of years ago. Anyhow, it dripped resin or sap, just gobs and gobs of it. When the sap got hard it became yellow or dark brown. People dig it up today when they can find it and call it amber. They make rings and necklaces of it.

"The sap dripped all over Old Smooth and Ugly. He was lazy, and he didn't take baths often. So the resin built up, and soon he had a shell of it. It covered that smooth skin of his, and I suppose he felt he looked better. Then he discovered that it kept him from getting sunburned and also kept off the cold wind at night. He had a portable house.

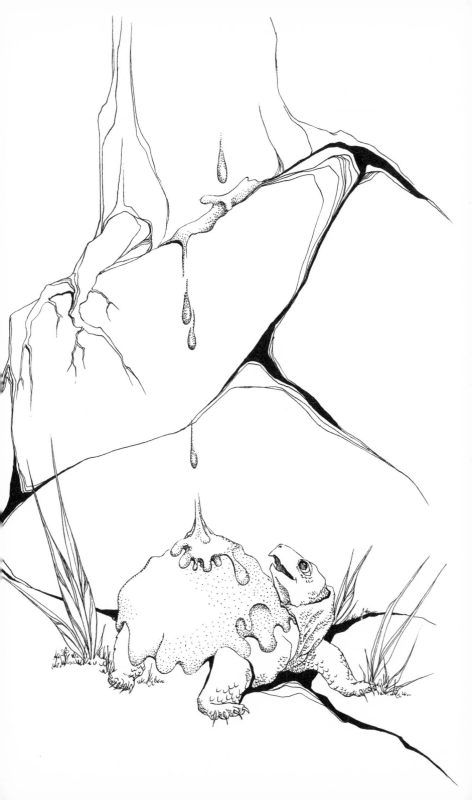

"The conference was about to break up with nothing decided when Old Smooth and Ugly walked up to the speaker's platform. 'I call this a shell,' he announced. 'It keeps the sun off and it keeps out the cold. It sheds the rain. Insects can't sting me when I'm asleep, and when it gets much thicker, I doubt if most animals will be able to eat me. About the only thing that can bother me is a big dinosaur. But they're disappearing fast, and in a few hundred years you won't see them except in museums. I suggest we all get shells.'

"Old Smooth and Ugly was the hero of the entire turtle world. He was given an honorary title, and a monument was built to him. They started calling him Old Mobile Home Herman. He married and had a great many descendants. Of course as time went by the shells became a part of us, and we became able to grow them. We box turtles, of course, have developed the best mobile homes. We can shut the doors of our shells front and back, and most turtles can't."

"My front shell won't close quite right," Wither-spoon said. "See?" He closed his front shell and then said something that sounded like "*Whumm, mumm, bump spin min blip.*"

"Don't try to talk with your shell closed," Aunt Myrtle said sharply. "You sound like an idiot."

"I said my front shell doesn't close right. The lower part bumps against the upper and leaves a little crack. A bee could sting me through that."

"I've said for some time you need orthodonture," Aunt Myrtle said. "I'll speak to your parents when they get home."

"What do I need?"

"To have your shell straightened. I think your front hinge got twisted when that nasty little girl kicked you last year. But it isn't serious."

"That was a great story," I said. "I'm glad that Old Smooth and Ugly invented shells."

"So are all turtles," Aunt Myrtle said. "It amuses me the way people think they have something new when we turtles have had it for centuries. The other day I heard a television station advertising motor homes as the latest thing, and I started to write a letter. Then I changed my mind. Why make people envious?"

 *two*

Witherspoon and I took an early morning walk over by Dillon Gymnasium, and we didn't see Aunt Myrtle until midafternoon. We bumped into her underneath a bush in front of the Joseph Henry House. We often find her there. She likes it because the Joseph Henry House is very old, and she says she feels more comfortable in colonial surroundings. She was half dozing in the afternoon sun.

"What's that on your chin?" Witherspoon asked.

"I don't know that anything is on my chin," Aunt Myrtle answered. "What does it look like?"

"Blood."

"It isn't blood," Aunt Myrtle said. "If it's red it must be strawberries."

"There aren't any ripe strawberries around," Witherspoon said. "Or if there are, you're keeping them a secret."

"I am well aware that there are no ripe strawberries in the immediate vicinity," Aunt Myrtle said haughtily. "Generally speaking, the faculty of Princeton University are miserable gardeners. I didn't say I had been eating ripe strawberries. I said that spot on my chin is probably strawberries."

"All right. How did it get there?"

"I have a friend," Aunt Myrtle said with a superior smile. "And this friend bakes delicious strawberry pies. She gave me some."

"Are cooked strawberries good?" I asked.

"Quite. I prefer fresh ones of course. I always prefer everything uncooked, from worms to peaches. But when the fresh article can't be had, the cooked will do quite nicely."

"Why do people cook things?" Witherspoon asked.

"I guess because they like them cooked," Aunt Myrtle said. "Humans have strange tastes."

"Gloria and I eat hamburger," Witherspoon said. "That's cooked."

"Yes, but we like it better when it's rare," I pointed out.

Students sometimes toss part of their hamburgers into the bushes on their way to class after lunch. If the hamburger is rare, Witherspoon and I eat it. I don't care much for mustard or pickles, which people seem to like for some strange reason. We never eat the bun from the hamburger either, but the birds do.

"The human taste makes no sense," Aunt Myrtle said. "I went to a lecture some days ago, and the professor said that several primitive tribes in Africa and Australia and South America eat insects and grubs. I wouldn't call that primitive. Those people appreciate the finer things in life. Can you explain why a person will eat a raw clam and turn up his nose at a nice juicy caterpillar?"

"I was in that delicatessen across Nassau Street, and they had cans of chocolate-covered ants for sale," Witherspoon said.

"You had better stay out of that delicatessen or they will have fresh turtle meat for sale," Aunt Myrtle warned. "But I agree that is a hopeful sign. Your Uncle Herman told me that one time when he was in North Africa, Casablanca I think it was, they had a plague of locusts. People caught them and fried them in hot fat like French fried potatoes. So maybe in time humans will discover again how delicious fresh insects are. Insects are willing to bite people. People ought to bite back."

"Uncle Herman went everywhere, didn't he?" I asked.

"Almost everywhere," Aunt Myrtle said proudly. "He was a restless soul. He always got along well with people, and often they took him along as a mascot. Of course turtles and humans generally get along well. Aside from the soup problem, we haven't any real quarrel with the human race. Now the woman who baked the strawberry pie is a nice lady and a friend. She often gives me fruits and pies."

"Where does she live?" Witherspoon asked.

"Oh, across Washington Road and on a ways. I'd visit her more often, but traffic has become such a problem. Actually she was your Uncle Herman's special friend. She feels quite indebted to Herman, and she should."

"Why?" I asked.

"It's a long story Gloria, and I wouldn't want to bore you two with it," she said. "Herman won a big prize for her in New York City."

Aunt Myrtle closed her eyes and waited for us to ask her to tell the story. She likes you to plead with her, but really she wants to tell the story all the time. Witherspoon is mean, I think. He won't say a word but just sits and grins and waits. I believe it is much nicer to make Aunt Myrtle feel we are anxious to hear her stories.

"I'd love to hear how Uncle Herman won the prize," I said. "Was it a turtle show? Like the dog shows they have?"

"Goodness, no," said Aunt Myrtle. "We turtles are too dignified and independent to take part in contests like that, especially if people were to draw up the rules. I ask you, what kind of a dog show is it when the dogs can't vote for the winner?"

"Then what sort of contest did Uncle Herman win?" Witherspoon asked.

"A baking contest. It was most unusual, but then Herman was a most unusual turtle."

"Tell us the story," I said in my sweetest voice.

"Well, since you both insist— To begin with, as you may recall, your Uncle Herman had initials carved in his back."

"I never saw Uncle Herman," Witherspoon objected.

"Nor me."

"What a pity!" Aunt Myrtle said. "He was a handsome turtle. Anyhow, years ago, in the early days of the university, a lovesick student saw Herman walking across the campus one day. He picked him up and took him to his room. Instead of studying as he should have, he spent an entire evening carving his girl friend's initials in Herman's back."

"Doesn't that hurt?" Witherspoon wanted to know.

"Not unless the carver goes through the shell," Aunt Myrtle said. "But it's nerve-racking, feeling that knife cutting into your shell. But your uncle was a man of steely nerves, and he didn't mind the carving so much. But he hated the initials. The girl's name was Yolande A. Murgatroyd. We never knew what the middle initial stood for."

"That spells YAM," I said.

"Exactly. That's a vegetable something like a sweet potato, in case you didn't know, Witherspoon. Herman never liked yams, and there he was with an advertisement for them carved into his back. However, in a way the initials were helpful. For some reason people feel kindly disposed toward a turtle who has initials carved in his back. Herman said it was the initials that first attracted the attention of Mrs. Gerber."

"Who is Mrs. Gerber?" I asked.

"The woman who baked the strawberry pie," Aunt Myrtle replied. "She has a beautiful flower garden. It's filled with perennials, and it has a little pool in it. There are a number of moist shady spots, and at times the scent from the various flowers is heavenly. Herman always liked to smell the flowers. Turtles, as everyone knows, are very cultured and appreciate the finer things. Herman, in addition to having an adventurous spirit, was a very sensitive turtle and loved beauty. So he spent a great deal of time in Mrs. Gerber's garden.

"Mrs. Gerber is a very gentle woman, and I'm sure she would have been friendly toward Herman anyhow, but the initials on his back interested her. She and Herman soon became friends and had a nice working arrangement. When she dug in the garden, Herman stayed nearby and ate any grubs she dug up. When she wasn't digging he ate insects. Herman was very fast and could reach out and catch the fastest flying insect in mid-air.

"Mrs. Gerber had poor eyes and had to wear very thick-lensed spectacles. If she dropped them she could see hardly anything. The trouble was that they were always falling off her nose when she leaned over. And of course no one can garden without leaning over. She would lose her glasses and have to fumble around in the dirt, feeling for them. One day Herman picked them up and practically put them in her hand. After that he found them regularly for her. She would call for him to help her. Of course she didn't know his real name was Herman. She called him Yam because of those initials. She would let him in the house, and he practically became a member of the family. But he really got in solid with her the day she lost her ring. It was damp, almost muddy, and she was setting out some plants. She took off her gloves to do something, and somehow her wedding ring came off with the glove. It fell among the plants. She was beside herself until Herman found the ring for her. We turtles have very sharp eyes as you know. You never see a turtle wearing glasses.

"After that Herman could do no wrong. She began feeding him all sorts of things. He had a sweet tooth and liked cookies and cakes and, above all, pies. He used to go into her kitchen and watch her bake. He got to know quite a bit about cooking.

"Mrs. Gerber is an outstanding cook, especially when it comes to pastry. Her neighbors are always asking her for advice, and several people have suggested that she write a cookbook. Anyhow, several years back there was a big baking contest sponsored by the May Baking Company. First a person had to submit a recipe to qualify. Then the contestant had to bake something and submit it to a local panel of judges. One hundred winners were picked from all over the United States to compete in a final baking contest in New York City. Each one had a stove and a place to work, and so on.

"Mrs. Gerber is a very quiet, shy woman, and she would never have thought of entering, but one of her neighbors sent in a recipe for her. This qualified her for the first round. Somehow friends persuaded her to bake something. Of course she won. This made her one of the final contestants. Herman heard people talking about it and became very interested. On the morning of the contest she set a basket of utensils and supplies on the back step while she went inside for something she had forgotten. Herman slipped into the basket and hid under a pie tin. He did things like that on impulse. Herman would go off to the South Pole on a minute's notice if he happened to feel in the mood. He never worried about how he would get back. Somehow he always did.

"Mrs. Gerber got to New York and began to unpack her basket, and there was Herman. She just laughed and put him on the work counter where he could watch. Herman said it was very exciting watching one hundred people getting ready to bake a pie or cake. There were ninety-two women and seven men in the final contest."

"That's only ninety-nine," Witherspoon said.

"One woman sprained her wrist rolling out a practice pie crust the night before," Aunt Myrtle said.

"As I was saying before I was interrupted by a silly remark, the ninety-nine people got ready to bake. There was a time limit—I've forgotten exactly what—but by a certain time everything had to be in the oven. Just as the contest was about to begin, Mrs. Gerber got called away to the telephone. It was a message about her mother who lived somewhere out west. She had fallen and broken her arm. By the time Mrs. Gerber got back she was already a few minutes behind everyone else, and she was nervous and upset because of the news.

"Herman said she did very well until she got to the upper crust of the pie. She had started to do the final rolling, when she dropped her glasses on the floor. She couldn't find them. Naturally none of the other contestants was going to stop what he or she was doing and help her. She got down on her knees and began feeling around on the floor. Herman was on top of the counter and couldn't get down to help. He saw that it was a real emergency. She was never going to get her pie finished in time.

"Your Uncle Herman was always a brilliant and resourceful turtle. He was at his best in an emergency. Most turtles would never have thought of what Herman did. He flipped over on his back and began rocking back and forth. He rolled that upper crust to just the right thickness, and then he dragged it in place on top of the pie. Mrs. Gerber found her glasses just as the bell rang. She got to her feet and discovered that the pie had somehow been finished. So she popped it into the oven.

"Well, she won the contest. She got a big sum of money and a complete set of equipment for a new kitchen. Her pie was judged the most delicious one in the contest. But what do you think really won for her? Remember there were one hundred excellent cooks there."

"Ninety-nine," Witherspoon corrected.

Aunt Myrtle ignored Witherspoon's remark.

"I don't know," I said. "What made her win?"

"That upper pie crust!" Aunt Myrtle said. "When Herman rolled around on his back, flattening out the dough, the initials on his back left raised letters in the crust. Of course they printed in reverse, and instead of saying 'YAM' they said 'MAY,' which was the name of the company sponsoring the contest."

"Pretty clever!" Witherspoon said. "That's what I call cool."

"And that is not all," Aunt Myrtle said. "As you may or may not know, when you make a two-crust pie, you have to pinch the top and bottom crust together. One of the judges said that Mrs. Gerber's pie had the most unusual design around the edge he had ever seen."

Aunt Myrtle paused and waited for Witherspoon or me to ask her what it was. Witherspoon was being stubborn again, so finally I asked.

"What was the design?"

"Herman went all around the pie and bit it together. His jaws left beautiful marks on the edge. He bit off any extra pieces of crust and ate them. Which was a good thing."

"Why?"

"Because that was the only bit of that pie he got. Those greedy judges ate every scrap!"

 *three*

Witherspoon and I went to a track meet at Palmer Stadium today. It was exciting but very confusing. A number of young men from a college named Yale came to Princeton for the meet. All those who took part in the meet wore special costumes. The Princeton men wore black shorts and orange jerseys, while the Yale men had costumes of blue and white. There was a large crowd watching, and they cheered and got very excited at times. Naturally Witherspoon and I were for Princeton since we live on the campus, but we never figured out what was supposed to be happening or why. Not much of it made any sense.

We saw Aunt Myrtle about dinnertime and explained that we had been to a track meet.

"I wondered where you were," she said. "I was going to suggest that we all go over to the faculty club for lunch. I saw them delivering a lot of hamburger there this morning. But it's just as well I didn't find you. I didn't stay. They made the hamburger into meat loaf, and I can't stand college meat loaf. And the conversation was boring. How was the track meet?"

"Noisy," I said.

"And we didn't understand what they were doing," Witherspoon said. "Why do they have track meets?"

"The human race does some strange things," Aunt Myrtle said. "And their athletic contests are among the strangest. They compete against each other. They struggle and struggle and get all excited, and finally one side or the other wins. But it never seems to settle anything. I guess they have very poor memories because the next year they go through the same rigmarole all over again. And the very same sort of contest too. However, even if I do think most athletic events are silly, I do know something about them. Your Uncle Herman was an authority on athletics, and I learned a great deal from him. Just what puzzled you about the track meet?"

"Well, a man took a long pole and then he ran like crazy," Witherspoon said. "Suddenly he stuck the end of the pole in the ground and went sailing up into the air. What was he trying to do? Fly?"

"He's pole vaulting," Aunt Myrtle said promptly. "He's trying to get high enough in the air to get over that bar that is perched between those two upright posts. He is supposed to get over without knocking down the bar."

"But he could walk right under the bar and get to the other side," Witherspoon pointed out.

"That is true. But the object is to go the highest and get to the other side."

"Sort of silly," Witherspoon said. "They land in the dirt and get all hot and tired. When they do get over they are right where they started."

"Witherspoon is right," I said. "They don't get anywhere in half the things they do in a track meet. A whole line of young men crouch down and then a gun goes off. They all run like mad but they go in a circle.

They finish right back where they started. The only thing they do is get out of breath."

"That seems an accurate description," Aunt Myrtle admitted. "Herman explained that to me one time. They are trying to see how fast they can do something. Don't ask me why. But it seems people think that speed is very important. Which it isn't, as any turtle can tell you. Maybe we ought to make a study of why people are so interested in speed. They are always making studies of things—like ants or ducks or cockroaches. If we studied them, we would find out why they do these strange things."

"Who cares?" Witherspoon asked.

"That is a good point," Aunt Myrtle said solemnly. "A very good point. Also we wouldn't learn much unless we could learn to think like people. And people can't learn much about turtles unless they can think like turtles. That, of course, is way beyond them since their brain has had only a million years or so to develop, while ours has been developing at least two hundred million years. People don't understand us. That's why you get silly stories like that one about the tortoise and the hare. You've both heard that tale, I suppose?"

"If you mean that story in Aesop's Fables, yes," Witherspoon said. "Gloria read it to me."

"Well everyone knows that story is ridiculous. Why would a tortoise race with a rabbit? Any turtle knows a hare is much faster, and he couldn't care less."

"Why did they have a race then?" I asked.

"They didn't. People just decided it was a race. Your

Uncle Herman knew both the rabbit and the turtle. You know a rabbit and a hare are slightly different. This was actually a rabbit, an Irish rabbit, in fact, by the name of Kevin O'Hare. The tortoise was named George II and was a distant cousin of Herman's. Anyhow, the tortoise and the rabbit were old friends. One day, quite by accident, they met some distance from home. George II had been traveling for several days, and so Kevin gave him the latest news, which was that Mrs. George II had stepped on a sharp stone and had cut her foot rather badly. George started home immediately because he was concerned. Kevin decided to go home at the same time. Even just loping along, he soon left George far behind. Then he stopped. But it wasn't because he got overconfident as the fable has it— he met an old friend, I think a girl friend, and he stopped to visit. After all *he* wasn't hurrying home to an injured wife. George II kept plodding along, and soon he passed Kevin. Kevin knew he was being passed, and he even called to George to tell his mother he might be late for dinner.

"There weren't any newspapers or TV newscasts in those days, but there were people around who could make a big story out of a little one just the same. Someone said there had been a race and that the turtle had won. Then people began seeing all sorts of morals or lessons from this so-called race about persistence and not becoming overconfident. Kevin and George II heard them and knew they were ridiculous, but they decided to say nothing. After all if people thought they had learned a valuable lesson from us animals, why not let them?"

"I doubt if even Mr. Aesop could have figured out any moral from that crazy pole vaulting," I said.

"I can," Witherspoon announced. "The higher you vault, the harder you fall."

"Not bad," Aunt Myrtle said approvingly. "I have hopes for you at times, Witherspoon. Your uncle preferred races to most sports. Crew was his favorite."

"What's that?" Witherspoon asked.

"It's a boat race. Have you seen those long narrow racing shells skimming over the water on Lake Carnegie?"

"I think I know what you mean," Witherspoon said. "I never saw one up close. I thought they were some kind of enormous water bugs with long legs."

"They do look like water bugs," Aunt Myrtle agreed. "Those are shells, and what you thought were legs are long oars. There are eight men in a crew who row and a coxswain who steers the boat and coaxes the others to row harder."

"Why?" I asked. "Lake Carnegie is just a little lake, and you could get across it in no time."

"And if they are in such a big hurry, why don't they go by car?" Witherspoon asked. "There's a bridge over the lake and a road right beside the shore."

"They aren't trying to get across the lake or to go up or down it. They are practicing to see how fast they can go. They don't really expect to go anywhere in a shell. If the water is very rough, they can't even go out in one."

The whole idea didn't make much sense, but I didn't say anything because I had a feeling she was about to tell a story. She gets a faraway look in her eye.

"Herman was quite fond of the water, much more so than most box turtles, and he used to stroll down to Lake Carnegie quite often and take a short dip. One day he went over to the boathouse. One of the students who was a member of a crew noticed him and those initials on his back. He picked him up and put him in the shell. This was the second or third crew, but that day they beat the varsity."

"What college is that?" Witherspoon asked.

"That isn't a college at all," I said. "It is the first or best team."

"Gloria is quite correct," Aunt Myrtle said. "But to get back to my story, Herman enjoyed riding in the shell, so he went down quite often after that. This same boy picked him up a number of times and put him in the shell, and each time they won. They adopted Herman as their mascot. They thought he brought them good luck. People are superstitious, you know.

"The following year the boy who was Herman's particular friend moved up to the varsity crew. He took Herman along on several races against other colleges, and each time Princeton won. One Saturday afternoon there was a race but there was also a concert at McCarter Theatre. A famous bassoon player was playing a solo, and I persuaded Herman to go to the concert instead of to the crew race. We both like the bassoon."

"What is a bassoon?" Witherspoon wanted to know.

"A musical instrument made of wood. You blow on

it and it produces a very deep sound. It's almost like a bullfrog's croaking. You know how lovely it is to hear a bullfrog croaking. Turtles are very musically inclined, and our family particularly so. Anyhow, we went to hear the bassoon. The theater was crowded, and we climbed all the way to the balcony to find a place where people wouldn't step on us.

"As we learned later, the crew was very upset when Herman didn't appear. They made hundreds of freshmen go out hunting for him. They went all over the campus calling 'Yam, Yam, come out, come out, wherever you am!'"

"I guess freshmen haven't studied English yet," I said.

"Oh, yes they have. But they love poetry, even bad poetry. They made such a noise around McCarter Theatre that the concert was interrupted. One violinist walked off the stage in a huff. While Herman's name isn't Yam, he knew they were looking for him. He started down the steps, slipped on the top one, and tumbled all the way to the bottom. He bounced off the last step and went bang into a man's wooden leg. Actually the false leg was aluminum, which is even harder. Herman was knocked out and his neck badly wrenched. He still tried to get to the crew house when he came to, but long before he got there the race was over. Princeton lost.

"Of course Herman and I knew that it didn't make any real difference who won or lost, but the crew was most unhappy. They were certain they had lost because Herman hadn't been there. People believe such silly things—that Friday the thirteenth is an unlucky day or that black cats are bad luck."

"Are black cats bad luck?" Witherspoon asked.

"Only if you are the cat," Aunt Myrtle said. "It's bad luck to be a cat in the first place instead of something sweet and lovely like a turtle. In the second place someone is apt to throw a rock at you because he thinks you are bad luck."

"Did Uncle Herman ever go out with the crew again?" I asked.

"Yes, indeed," Aunt Myrtle said. "He won the great race with Cornell for them. I've forgotten what year that was. It's hard to keep track as it never seems to be settled. They keep on racing no matter who wins. But they feel it is important each year, and Herman liked the crew that year, especially this one boy."

"How did Herman win the race?" Witherspoon asked. "He couldn't pull an oar."

"Well, when the kink had worked out of his neck, he went down to the boathouse again. They were overjoyed. They fed him all sorts of things and took him out to practice with them every day. They talked about nothing but this race with Cornell. It seems that Cornell is an extra-special rival of Princeton's."

"Where is Cornell?" I asked.

"It's up north in Ithaca, New York. It has a beautiful campus, and there is a big lake nearby. I went up for a visit many years ago and spent the winter. When I came up in the spring at my usual time, there were at least four feet of snow. I'll take Princeton any time."

"Why don't people hibernate in the winter?" Witherspoon asked.

"It would certainly be the sensible thing for them to do," Aunt Myrtle said thoughtfully. "It would save the expense of heating the house all winter and all that fuss over fur coats, galoshes, and lost mittens. I guess it is because they like speed. They get on snowmobiles and skis and zip around freezing their noses and breaking their legs. Of course down in Florida they don't have any snow, and the turtles stay awake and the people sleep on the beaches."

"What happened at the Cornell race?" I reminded her.

"That's right, I never finished my story, did I? The day before the race they locked Herman in a pen. It wasn't a nice thing to do, but they didn't mean to be unkind. They wanted to be certain that he would be there for the race. They fed him a whole raw hamburger. Herman liked hamburger, and he ate it all. He was still sleeping when they came to get him for the race the next day.

"Once he was out on the lake, he woke up, of course. The crew was very worried. One man had got a bad cold, and a substitute was rowing in his place. It wasn't that the new man wasn't good, but the crew had been rowing together for so long that they were uneasy about a change. With a new man they might not row as smoothly. If a crew has a ragged stroke, it hasn't a chance of winning. Also, according to the records, Cornell was a little faster than Princeton that year. The whole crew was upset and Herman sensed it.

"As they were rowing toward the starting line, one man got a cramp in his leg, and that really bothered them. Herman knew that unless they settled down, they would never win. As they were waiting for the starting gun he realized that something had to be done. I think I mentioned before how resourceful Herman was. He saw an opportunity, so he dived over the side and started swimming toward the Cornell shell.

"Several men in the Princeton crew saw him slip into the water, and they were afraid that he had deserted them and that their luck had gone with him. But Herman's special friend suspected that he was up to something. Herman swam as fast as he could and arrived at the Cornell shell just in the nick of time. The crew was leaning forward with their oars in the water, ready to pull at the sound of the starting gun. Just as the gun went off, Herman reached up and clamped his jaws on the edge of one of the oars.

"Naturally, the man couldn't row properly with a heavy turtle hanging on his oar. In fact he couldn't keep in stroke with the others. Herman was able to hold on for only three strokes, but that was enough. It got the whole Cornell crew in an uproar, and before they could get rowing smoothly again, Princeton was in the lead by four lengths. Cornell never caught up.

"Cornell complained bitterly to the judges, and two Cornell men swore they saw a turtle hanging from that oar. They said Princeton had managed it somehow, and they claimed a foul. The Princeton crew all kept straight faces and said that was the silliest story they had ever heard. The judges looked at the Cornell oar. It was painted a bright red on a diagonal. Red is Cornell's color. Herman had scraped off some of the paint, he had clamped down so hard on that oar. One of the judges inspected the marks and said they didn't look like they had been made by a turtle's teeth. They called in a professor of zoology who pointed out that turtles don't have teeth. He said he couldn't imagine why a turtle would try to eat an oar, even a snapping turtle. The judges decided the whole story was nonsense, and Princeton was judged the winner.

"Your Uncle Herman was a hero. The only trouble was that he wasn't there. He was still a mile or so down the lake. When he was whipped around on the end of that oar, it wrenched his neck again, and he could hardly move. It took him two days to swim ashore and walk back to the boathouse. When he did finally appear there was a great welcoming celebration. Some of the red paint from the Cornell oar was still on his lower jaw, and even those of the crew who hadn't seen him grab the oar were convinced. They started to raise money to build a statue to honor Herman but had to drop the idea."

"Why?" Witherspoon asked.

"It seems it is just as important to win fairly as to win," Aunt Myrtle said. "People have something they call sportsmanship. Now they hadn't done anything un-fair—a turtle had. So it was all right to win, but they couldn't admit why. So the statue was never built."

 *four*

Witherspoon and I went down to Lake Carnegie this morning to look at the boathouse and the racing shells that Aunt Myrtle had told us about yesterday. We took a short dip in the lake and were on our way back when we met Alphonso. Alphonso is a woodchuck. We've known him for two years. The last time I saw him was back in April, and he was terribly thin. Today he looked fat and sleek.

"You've put on a lot of weight, haven't you?" Witherspoon asked Alphonso.

"Quite a bit," Alphonso said, proudly. "If I keep on I'll hardly be able to waddle come October."

Witherspoon went over and peeked in Alphonso's house, which is a hole in the ground. "What are you doing, digging a new entrance?" he asked.

"No, just enlarging that one," Alphonso said. "It was getting a bit tight, I've gained so much. And when one of those big German shepherds happen along, I like to be able to dive out of danger fast."

"What have you been eating that is making you so fat?" Witherspoon asked.

"Beans, peas, carrot tops, lettuce, all sorts of vegetables," Alphonso said. "You know this year's crop of new professors at Princeton are some of the best gardeners in years. There's three wonderful stands of corn coming along. Much earlier than usual."

"Spring was early this year," I said.

"True," Alphonso said. "Quite true. Just as we predicted." He stuck his chest out and looked very pompous.

"Who predicted?" Witherspoon asked.

"We woodchucks," Alphonso said. "We always predict when spring will come. I thought everybody knew that."

"That's the first I heard about it," Witherspoon said. He wasn't trying to be nasty, but sometimes Witherspoon isn't too tactful.

"I imagine there are lots of things a youngster like you hasn't heard," Alphonso said. "Besides, you are sound asleep when we woodchucks are up and about making predictions about spring."

I'd never heard anything about woodchucks making predictions either, and I didn't like the uppity way Alphonso was talking to my brother. I'll admit that Witherspoon is not as smart or as educated as I am, but he's a very bright turtle and certainly a lot smarter than a fat old woodchuck.

"There's lots of things Witherspoon doesn't know about ground*hogs*," I agreed in a very sweet voice. "But that's mainly because he's never been much interested in ground*hogs*."

Alphonso was very annoyed. He didn't say a word but just stalked away and started eating a clump of clover. I motioned to Witherspoon and we went on back toward Pyne Hall.

"He doesn't like being called a groundhog, does he?"

Witherspoon asked when we were far enough away. "Why?"

"I don't know," I said. "But I remember Aunt Myrtle saying that if you wanted to insult a woodchuck, just call him a groundhog."

We were passing the gymnasium when we met Aunt Myrtle. She was stretched out in the sun at the edge of a shrub border. "Nice place for a siesta," she said. "And every now and then a bug flies by. Why don't you join me for a while?"

We weren't really going any place, so we stretched out beside Aunt Myrtle. After a few minutes, Witherspoon remembered Alphonso.

"Why does a woodchuck get mad when you call him a groundhog?" he asked.

"Well, everyone is sensitive about what he's called. Look how busy people are inventing new names for themselves. The garbage men want to be called sanitation men these days, and janitors want to be called custodians. A woodchuck doesn't like being called any kind of a pig or hog. But they have been putting on airs for a long, long time now."

"They look like fat pigs, and they do live in the ground," Witherspoon said.

"That is a very acute observation," Aunt Myrtle agreed. "In some places they used to be called whistle pigs because they look like pigs and they whistle. But this doesn't make any difference to them. They want to be called woodchucks."

"They don't chuck any wood around," I objected.

"The Indians called them *Ot-choeck* or something like that," Aunt Myrtle explained. "The white man got it mixed up and it became 'woodchuck.' The scientific people here at the college call them marmots. But I'm quite satisfied to call them groundhogs. Sort of keeps them in their place."

"You said they had been putting on airs," I said. "What about?"

"Alphonso said he was busy predicting the weather while I was still asleep," Witherspoon said. "What did he mean?"

"Ordinarily I would remind you that it is polite to let your sister's question be answered before you butt in and ask one," Aunt Myrtle said. "But in this case I will forgive you because the two questions can be answered at one time. It just so happens I am an authority on the groundhog's so-called ability to tell when spring will come. And I can tell you definitely that their claim is one of the greatest hoaxes of all time."

An ant tickled Witherspoon on the tail, and he turned around to see what it was. Aunt Myrtle insists that everyone pay absolute attention when she tells one of her stories, and I could see that she was annoyed.

"Some time when you are not in such a hurry and can listen politely instead of fidgeting, I might be persuaded to tell you the whole story," Aunt Myrtle said.

"I wasn't fidgeting," Witherspoon said. "Something bit my tail. I think it was an ant."

"Those ants!" Aunt Myrtle said. "Busy busy busy! They're as bad as people. Always rushing somewhere.

Thank heaven we turtles take a more sensible approach to life. Someday I'll tell you about a colony of ants that almost wrecked Nassau Hall."

"What about the woodchucks?" I asked. Sometimes Aunt Myrtle gets off on a second story right in the middle of another and you never hear the end of the first one.

"Oh, yes, the groundhogs," Aunt Myrtle said. "Well, many years ago, there used to be a number of groundhogs right here on the main campus. Groundhogs have always been like us turtles, quite willing to let man move in as long as he leaves us a reasonable amount of room. The trouble between man and groundhogs is caused by those great big holes groundhogs dig. Back in the days before automobiles, everyone either rode a horse or drove a horse and wagon. And every now and then a horse stepped in a big woodchuck hole and broke his leg. Naturally the owner of the horse didn't like that at all. Groundhogs have never been too popular here on the campus. But there were some. One of Alphonso's ancestors, a groundhog by the name of Alexander, had a burrow under the edge of a stone wall near one of the student halls. The building has since been torn down, but that doesn't matter. A student named Calthrop had a room with a window that looked right down on the main entrance to Alexander's home." Aunt Myrtle paused and looked first at Witherspoon and then at me. "Have you ever visited a groundhog's burrow?"

"No," I said. Witherspoon shook his head.

"You should," Aunt Myrtle said. "It is very interesting. A groundhog takes life very easy and does little but eat and sleep. The one exception is his burrow. He digs and digs and digs. He is an expert mining engineer. His main entrance drops straight down about three feet and then makes a turn. His second entrance or back door usually slopes down more gradually. His burrow winds around and goes up and down so that water that goes in either entrance never finds its way into his living room where he sleeps. Sometimes in very cold places like New England, he may be ten feet under the ground. And one entrance may be seventy-five feet from the other. He has very sharp claws, and he can dig fast. When a dog or a person tries to dig him up, he can usually dig a tunnel and fill it up behind himself faster than they can follow."

"Groundhogs sleep all winter the way we do, don't they?" Witherspoon asked.

"Yes, they do. That is called hibernating. And that is the only sensible thing to do in the winter. As I said the other day, I have never figured out why humans, who think they are so intelligent, haven't learned to hibernate. They wouldn't have to go out in all that cold gray weather, and they wouldn't have to shovel snowy sidewalks."

"But you said they go where it's warm like the birds do," I reminded her.

"Some, but usually just for a week or two. And that's expensive and a lot of trouble. They have to pack their clothes and travel a long way to a warm place like Florida, and when they get there it's jammed. It's much, much simpler to just dig down in the ground a foot or two the way we do, or go down in your burrow the way groundhogs do, and sleep until the weather turns better. But whatever the silly reason, people stay awake all winter.

"To get back to my story, this student by the name of Herbie Calthrop could look out of his window and see the entrance to Alexander's burrow. They became sort of friends. Young Calthrop didn't bother Alexander, and naturally Alexander didn't bother him. Alexander was one of the few groundhogs left around the college buildings.

"It seems a dean's wife, I've long since forgotten her name, was on her way to church one Sunday morning. She was wearing a new pink dress and hat. It was in the spring and some groundhog had just dug a new entrance to his burrow. It was badly placed and came out in the middle of a stretch of lawn. The dean's wife was taking a short cut and had her nose high in the air because of her new clothes. She stepped in the hole and fell flat on her face. She sprained her ankle and, to make matters worse, ruined her new dress. She raised such a fuss that they tried to get rid of all the woodchucks. Alexander was one of the few they missed.

"One of the men who worked around the grounds, his first name was Peter, was from New England. He was fond of woodchucks, and he didn't bother Alexander either. When Peter was working around this particular building, he and this student Calthrop used to talk. One day they were discussing woodchucks, and your Uncle Herman and I happened to be nearby.

" 'How does he know when it's spring and it's time to come up out of that hole?' Herbie Calthrop asked.

" 'I suppose he's got some sort of a built-in clock,' Peter said. 'I used to watch them when I was on the farm in New Hampshire. Along about the end of February or early March, they'd appear. When we had an early spring they'd come out early. Maybe the temperature has something to do with it.'

" 'A woodchuck is pretty far down to feel any difference in temperature,' Herbie Calthrop pointed out.

" 'Maybe you ought to make a study of when and why woodchucks come out in the spring,' Peter suggested. 'Write a book about it. There seem to be books about everything else.'

" 'Maybe I will,' Herbie Calthrop said. 'I'll quote you as an expert.'

" 'You should have known my dog Rover,' Peter said. 'Rover seemed to know when groundhogs were about to come out, and he'd be waiting. They're very sleepy, and they move slowly when they first appear. He could catch them easily even when he got old and slow himself. That dog knew more about woodchucks than any person who ever lived. He was a real expert. He could have written a book!' "

Aunt Myrtle smiled a very superior smile. "Of course none of them knew half as much as Herman and I did about why a woodchuck comes out in the spring. He does have a sort of time clock, but mainly he's like turtles. He puts on fat in the summer and fall and this is used up while he sleeps during the winter. If he has lots of fat he can sleep later. If he doesn't have such a big supply, he wakes up earlier. He's hungry!

"That winter we happened to burrow down into the

ground near Alexander's burrow. Actually Herman had spent several winters in that part of the campus and so had I. It was really our home territory and Alexander was a newcomer. Anyhow, Alexander's bedroom happened to be nearer the surface than usual, and Herman and I happened to burrow deeper. We were quite near each other. It was a miserable winter—the most uncomfortable I have ever spent. Alexander snored, a long whistling snore, and it was annoying. I had a terrible time getting to sleep at all. Then to make matters worse, just before he turned in for the winter, Alexander had discovered the vegetable garden of a Professor Amalfi who taught Italian literature. It was filled with garlic, and Alexander absolutely stuffed himself on garlic. I don't mind garlic too much, but Herman hated the smell of it. Some sort of crack opened up in the soil, and Alexander's breath seeped through to where we were sleeping. The snores got louder and the place reeked of garlic, which upset Herman. He was in a terrible rage. On February 2, he dug his way through to where Alexander was sleeping. He tried to wake Alexander, but waking a hibernating woodchuck is practically impossible. Herman shook him, kicked him, stepped on him, and hissed in his ear, but Alexander paid no attention and just kept breathing garlic in Herman's face.

"Herman climbed up the tunnel to the surface and looked out. It was a bright, sunny day but cold and windy. It was much too early to stay up, as Herman realized after one glance around.

" 'If you'll help me, I'll push him up to the surface and let that wind blow a little of the garlic smell away,' he suggested.

"Together we pushed and pushed and finally got Alexander up the tunnel. He was all curled up in a ball, and we half rolled him along. When we got him to the surface Herman turned him around so that his nose was facing the wind. I happened to look up and there was Herbie Calthrop peering from his window.

"We left Alexander there with his nose just above ground. We planned to go back and get him in a few minutes, but we didn't have to. That bright sun shining in his eyes must have bothered him. Woodchucks are half blind when they first wake up, and light bothers them. He was never really awake, but he turned around by himself and went back to where he had been sleeping. He smelled a little less like a garlic clove, and I guess he changed his position because he didn't snore so. We all went back to sleep for six weeks. I heard later that it snowed and the wind blew the entire time. It was a very cold, wintry February, and the snow didn't melt until well into March.

"Alexander, Herman, and I all came out the first real warm day. I don't think Herbie Calthrop saw us, but he did notice Alexander. It so happened that he was supposed to write a paper for some course, probably biology, and he had done no work on it at all. It was due the next day. He sat up very late that night and wrote it. It was a warm night for March, and he had the window open slightly. Your Uncle Herman and I

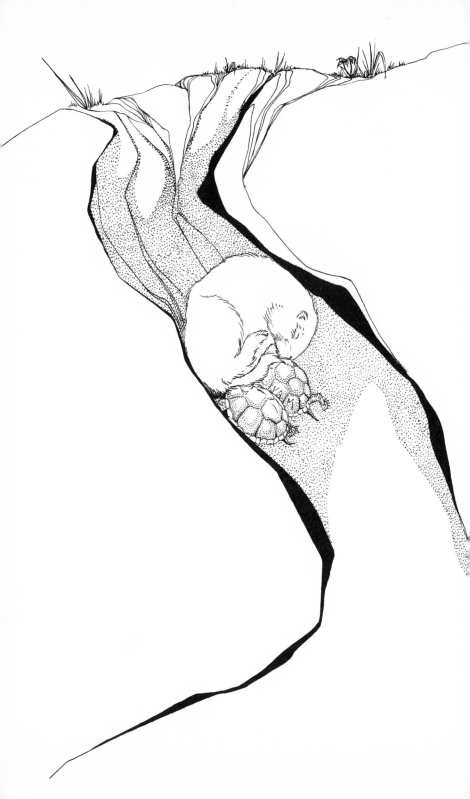

were right beneath the window, and we listened to him read the paper to a friend.

"That boy Herbie Calthrop didn't care much for hard work but he had a vivid imagination. There were only three facts in his entire paper. (1) A woodchuck had poked his head out of his hole on February 2. That was when Herman and I pushed Alexander up. (2) The sun was shining and Alexander went back down. (3) Six weeks later it was spring and Alexander came out again. So Herbie Calthrop came up with the silly idea that woodchucks poked their heads out of their holes on February 2, which he called Groundhog Day, and that if they saw their shadow they would go back inside, and there would be six weeks more of bad winter weather. He quoted Peter Gardener as an authority and said that extended research by a Professor Rover confirmed this. He said Professor Rover had observed woodchucks closely most of his adult life. He didn't mention that Rover was a dog.

"The professor who read the paper had a friend who ran a newspaper. This man thought Calthrop's paper was unusual, so he published it. Other papers picked it up, and soon everyone was saying that February 2 was Groundhog Day and that groundhogs were good prophets of the weather. Lots of superstitious people believed it, and when the groundhogs heard it, they did too. They began to act very important and stuffy and went around saying that they could predict spring. That silly pompous Alexander began calling himself Alexander the Great. He was so conceited that he was impossible. The silly idiot wouldn't even admit that Herman and I had pushed him up to the surface on February 2. He was so sleepy that he didn't remember what happened."

"And from that one time, people still say February 2 is Groundhog Day?" I asked.

"Well, that's most of the story but not quite all," Aunt Myrtle said. "Alexander was so taken with the idea that he was a weather prophet that he decided he would appear next February 2. He had his mind all made up when he went to sleep that fall. You can do that, you know, if you decide to wake up at a certain time. And I'll give him credit, the next February 2 he did appear. Herbie Calthrop's paper had aroused a great deal of interest, and a whole group had gathered in his window. There were three professors and the editor of the local paper. Sure enough Alexander appeared. It was a cold, gray day, much too cold for anyone except humans to be up and around, but Alexander was so determined to live up to his publicity that he went outside his hole, sat up straight for some time and even whistled. He was so excited he couldn't sleep, and he stayed outside all day. The sun was not out so he didn't see his shadow.

"All the people watching were very excited. I think humans *like* to believe in silly superstitious stories. Anyhow, Alexander's appearance was recorded in all the newspapers. And it just happened we had a very early spring that year so Herbie Calthrop added on to his story that if the groundhog did not see his shadow winter would be short. Hundreds of times since the groundhog's so-called prophecy has been wrong, but people still repeat the same silly story."

"How did Alexander act after this second time?" Witherspoon asked. "He must have been really famous then."

"He never knew," Aunt Myrtle said. "You see he stood up in that cold wind so long that February 2 that he got pneumonia. He wasn't alive to enjoy the early spring that he predicted. And to tell you the truth I didn't feel too sorry. I don't think I could have stood another summer of his boasting."

 *five*

*A*unt Myrtle promised last summer to take us through the university chapel, but we postponed it for one reason or another, and it was yesterday when we finally got around to it. The chapel has big, heavy doors, and naturally we had to wait until these were open. We found them open yesterday morning, so we walked in and made a complete tour of the chapel. Aunt Myrtle pointed out what she thought were the nicest windows, and Witherspoon almost sprained his neck looking up at them and at the high ceiling.

"They must have built this for very tall people," he said.

"Don't be silly," I told him. "People are never that tall."

"Then why did they build it this way?" Witherspoon asked. He can think of more questions than any turtle I know.

"Just because they do," I said.

"That's not a reason."

"He's right," Aunt Myrtle said. "I guess it is to make the building impressive so that people will feel solemn. It probably makes the organ sound better, and it makes the building cool and comfortable in the summer."

She was correct about that. It was the coolest spot we'd found, so we went over in the corner and took a nap. When we woke up someone had closed the door, and we had to spend the night there. We weren't worried though, because we knew someone would come sooner or later and open the door. They did early the next morning. However, we didn't leave because we discovered they were having a wedding at ten thirty.

The wedding was very interesting. Lots and lots of people came and sat in the seats in the front of the chapel. Meanwhile the organ played soft music, which was very nice. All the people were dressed in their fanciest clothes. Then finally the music got much louder, and eight girls in blue dresses, all carrying flowers, walked slowly down the aisle. They were followed by a very pretty young woman wearing a white dress and carrying a big bouquet of flowers. She was escorted by an older man who Aunt Myrtle said was her father. When the bride got to the altar, a young man came over from one side and stood beside her. The minister asked something and they answered. I couldn't hear it all, but finally the minister said, "I pronounce you man and wife." Then they turned and left the church, and soon everyone else did too. We were the last ones out.

"Where are they going?" Witherspoon asked.

"To a reception, I imagine," Aunt Myrtle said. "They have that in a big room somewhere—sometimes a hotel. Everyone congratulates the bride and groom, and then they all have something to eat and drink."

"That sounds like the best part of the wedding to me," Witherspoon said. He is always hungry.

"They don't have anything very good at receptions," Aunt Myrtle said. "No raw meat or juicy bugs. Just silly little sandwiches usually, junk like egg salad and fish between thin slices of bread."

"I thought the wedding was very nice," I said. "The bride was pretty."

"It *was* a nice wedding," Aunt Myrtle admitted. "But sort of routine. Not nearly as exciting as some weddings in this chapel. It isn't often that there is a wedding like the one Herman and I saw."

"When was this wedding?" I asked. "And where?"

"Right here," Aunt Myrtle said. "But it was many years ago. Back about 1910 or some time like that. Styles and lots of things were much different then."

"You mean they didn't wear fancy clothes?" I asked. "I thought the dresses were pretty."

"Oh, the clothes were much the same, but people's ideas were different. You see almost all the women had long hair. The few who cut their hair short were considered very daring, and many people said no nice girl would ever cut her hair."

"That's funny," Witherspoon said. "Now lots of boys have long hair, and lots of girls cut theirs short."

"That's right, and people object to that too," Aunt Myrtle said. "Anyhow, the girl who was getting married at the wedding I am discussing was named Millicent Sandford, and she had cut her hair quite short. She did it as a protest."

"Protest against what?" I asked.

"She was a very active suffragette."

"What's that?" Witherspoon asked. "Some sort of a professor?"

"I guess I'd better explain," Aunt Myrtle said. "You see people are centuries and centuries behind turtles. I have no idea if girl turtles ever had to struggle for their rights. If they did it was ages ago, and no one even remembers. As far as I know boy and girl turtles have always been on an equal footing. But people are different. Women in many places of the world have really no rights at all. Men run everything. I suppose women have always been better off here in the United States than in most parts of the world, but for a long time they still didn't have the same rights as men. Back when this wedding took place they could not vote."

"Vote for what?" Witherspoon asked.

"Oh, for president of the United States, for their senators or representatives, for the governor, or even for the mayor of the town. A few states allowed women to vote, but most of them didn't. So a group of women organized to change this. They made speeches, wrote papers, marched in the streets, talked to lawmakers, and other things. They called themselves suffragettes. Of course there were other women who felt that no nice girl would be a suffragette. But Millicent Sandford was a suffragette and proud of it. She worked very hard to win women the vote. She cut off her long hair as a protest to show that she felt women had a right to do what they wanted with their hair, just as men did with their hair and beards. The man she was marrying claimed he didn't care whether she had short hair or long hair. His name was Jonathan Slurp. He came from a wealthy family who thought they were very important. I believe they were the Long Island Slurps. Now Jonathan was worried about his mother and father. They were quite old-fashioned, and he was certain they would disapprove of Millicent's short hair. He persuaded her to wear a wig for the wedding. She didn't like the idea very much, but since they expected to move to Colorado after their wedding she finally agreed. Of course with all the veil and headdress no one could ever guess she was wearing a wig, so she didn't expect any trouble.

"Everything went wrong from the moment the wedding started. To begin with the minister came to the entrance of the chapel before the ceremony. He went outside to say something to someone. On his way back he tripped."

63

"On what?" Witherspoon asked.

"Well, over Herman as a matter of fact," Aunt Myrtle said. "We were hurrying to get inside and were near the door. But the minister should have seen us. He must have been very clumsy. Anyhow, he fell on the stone steps and cut a huge gash in his forehead. They had to rush him off to the hospital. Most of the people were already inside, and they all had to wait while they found a substitute minister. This upset the Slurps no end because the minister who had fallen was an old friend. It was Saturday and although they have a divinity school in Princeton, they had a difficult time finding another minister. The fishing was excellent in those days, and most everyone had gone fishing. They did finally find a young graduate student who agreed to perform the ceremony.

"It took about half an hour for the substitute minister to arrive, and everyone was tired of waiting. One man in one of the rear pews went sound asleep. He had one foot stuck out in the aisle. One shoe either had a nail sticking out of it or one of those metal plates that you sometimes see on the toes and heels of shoes. The wedding finally started, and Millicent was walking down the aisle, somewhat faster than usual to make up for the lost time, when her long wedding veil snagged on this man's shoe. Naturally, it pulled on her headdress and pulled her wig around until the hair was hanging over her face. She was a calm and cool young lady. All the people around gasped. Some of them were very shocked to see that she had short hair, but she didn't seem flustered. She simply pulled her wig back straight and looked down to see what had caught her veil. The man was still sleeping. In fact he began to snore. Millicent had a very hot temper. She reached over and shook him.

" 'If you will kindly disentangle your big feet from my veil, we will be able to proceed with the wedding,' she said in a clear loud voice.

"Some people gasped and some laughed. The young minister tried to keep his face straight, but he didn't quite manage. This annoyed the Slurps, who were already quite shocked by their daughter-in-law's short hair. They thought both Millicent and the minister should be dignified and solemn.

"Herman and I were about halfway toward the altar. I was quite satisfied with our location since we had a nice safe spot under a pew where no one was kicking us or stepping on us. But Herman wanted to go nearer the front so he could see better. He waited until Millicent had passed and then stepped out into the aisle himself. She had a long train on her wedding gown that was dragging along behind her. As I have said, Herman is a quick thinker. He decided he might as well ride, so he simply stepped onto her train.

"Naturally, having a good-sized box turtle riding on your wedding train doesn't make walking any easier, but Millicent managed. Some man who was sitting next to the aisle saw Herman. I suppose he thought he would be helpful. He half got to his feet and leaned out to grab Herman. He leaned too far and fell smack on Millicent's train. There was a horrible rip, and the train began to tear. Millicent had to stop. She turned around and saw this man getting up from the aisle. She also saw that her train was almost torn off about six inches above the floor.

" 'I'm certainly not going to drag you to the altar,' she said. She turned, hitched up her dress, and tore the train off the rest of the way. She left it there and calmly went toward the altar again as though nothing had happened.

"Herman escaped from the man, and he went on toward the front of the chapel too. However, he stayed out of the aisle, threading his way under the benches until he got to the front. He stopped under the front pew right beneath Mrs. Slurp, the groom's mother.

"Mrs. Slurp had slipped off her shoes. I guess they were too tight and pinched her toes."

"Why do people wear shoes at all?" Witherspoon asked.

"In the winter their feet get cold," Aunt Myrtle explained. "I really don't know why they wear them in the summer. Some children and some young people don't. But back then the women all wore shoes. Some even wore high shoes that buttoned up around their ankles. For some strange reason women often get shoes that are too tight. I've heard it's because they want their feet to look small, but that's silly. Any intelligent turtle knows that big feet are not only beautiful but much better to dig with. But to get back to my story, Mrs. Slurp had slipped off her shoes, and she sat there wiggling her toes. She was an excitable woman, and several things had already happened to make her feel nervous.

"Herman said later that those wiggling toes kept blocking his view, and they made *him* nervous. Finally they got too much for him, and he reached out and bit her little toe. He bit it hard and she screamed. She looked down; she saw just his head as he backed away under the seat. Then she really screamed.

" 'A snake!' she screeched and jumped up on the seat. 'I've been bitten by a snake!'

"Everyone went into a panic. Women jumped on seats and some men did too. Others rushed around trying to look brave, and the whole place was in an uproar. Most of the people in back ran for the doors. Mrs. Slurp, after screaming and jumping up on the seat, suddenly fainted. Someone caught her just in time to keep her from falling on her head. Jonathan Slurp left his place beside Millicent and rushed over to his mother. She began to come to, and a bit of quiet came back to the chapel. Jonathan went back to the altar and said, 'We'll have to postpone the ceremony. Mother is too upset to go on.'

" 'Your mother isn't the one getting married,' Millicent said. 'But I think maybe we'd better postpone it. Indefinitely.'

"She stalked down the aisle and out of the church. A big group of people were milling around outside, not knowing what to do. Several of them asked her if they should go back inside.

" 'No. There's not going to be a wedding,' she said.

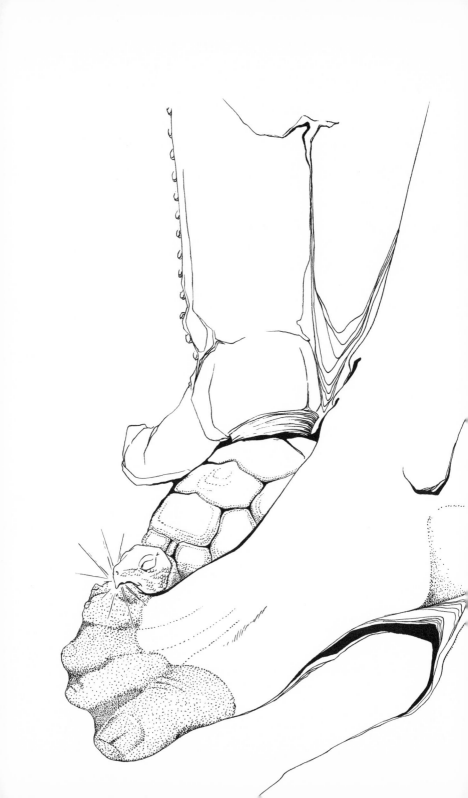

'But it's a shame to go to all this trouble and get all you fine people together and not have anything happen!' She yanked off her wig and handed it to someone. 'I'd like your attention for a few minutes,' she called. 'There are a few facts I would like to present as to why women should have the same right to vote as men.'

"She made a fine speech. Some of the people cheered, and of course some made remarks and catcalls. Right in the middle of her talk the young minister appeared with a box for her to stand on so she could see her audience better. Toward the end Mr. and Mrs. Slurp came out of the chapel. When Mrs. Slurp saw who was giving the speech, she fainted again."

"That sounds like a real wow of a wedding," Witherspoon said. "I wish today's had been like that."

"Did Millicent ever marry Jonathan?" I asked.

"No, she didn't," Aunt Myrtle said. "As a matter of fact about a week later she eloped with that young minister."

 *six*

Witherspoon disappeared this morning. He wandered off somewhere by himself. Aunt Myrtle and I went for a short swim in the big pool by the Woodrow Wilson building. Then we found a nice secluded spot and let the sun dry us off. Aunt Myrtle started talking about nothing in particular. She calls it "philosophizing." She says that when a student goes to college and doesn't know what else to be, he becomes a philosopher. When she doesn't really have anything to talk about, she philosophizes.

"Sometimes I have hopes for people," Aunt Myrtle said. "Take this nice fountain, for example. Just think how much nicer the world would be if they built more of these and fewer parking lots. And have you noticed what they did with that new addition to the Firestone Library?"

"I noticed it was a mess for a long, long time," I said.

"Yes, it was, but that isn't what I meant," Aunt Myrtle said. "What I meant was that they built most of it under the ground. Maybe humans are learning that being underground is a good idea, at least in the winter."

Witherspoon appeared just then, and whatever Aunt Myrtle was going to say she didn't finish. "Where have you been?" she asked Witherspoon.

"I went to a lecture," Witherspoon said. "I didn't mean to go, but one of the students picked me up and stuck me in his pocket. He sat near the front, so I heard the whole lecture."

"How did you get away?" I asked.

"Toward the end of the lecture he put me in a girl student's purse. She was very nice. She put me down on the ground when she left the hall."

"What was the lecture about?" Aunt Myrtle asked. "I hope something that improved your mind."

"It was about mountaineering," Witherspoon said. "The man who gave the lecture had climbed a big high mountain called Annapurna. It's in the Himalayas, wherever they are."

"The Himalayas are a very high range of mountains in southern China and Nepal. Nepal, for your information, is on the northern border of India. I do wish you two would go to a few classes on geography."

"I don't think they teach geography at Princeton," I said.

"Possibly you're right," Aunt Myrtle admitted. "That may be why you see so many people walking around the campus looking as though they don't know where they're going. Anyhow, tell us about the lecture, Witherspoon."

"There isn't much to tell. This man and five others set out to climb to the top of Annapurna. They climbed and climbed and it got colder and colder. They had to camp in the snow, and they had all sorts of terrible things happen. A blizzard almost blew them away, they ran out of food, one man slipped down in a big crack in the ice and died, the speaker froze his toes, but finally they got to the top."

"Then what happened?" I asked.

"Nothing," Witherspoon said. "They came down again, and they slipped and they slid and they fell half the way down."

"Why did they climb it?" I asked.

Witherspoon shrugged his shoulders. When a turtle does that his whole shell has to shrug. "That's the one thing the speaker didn't explain," Witherspoon said. "He had slides showing different parts of the climb. But he didn't show one of the top, and he didn't say what they found up there. That's why I came looking for Aunt Myrtle. Why do people climb mountains?"

Aunt Myrtle hung her head. "I am ashamed to admit that I don't know," she said. "But the only thing to do when you don't know something is to admit it. Even your Uncle Herman was never able to figure out why people climbed mountains. And he tried to learn. He went to greater lengths than any turtle in history has ever gone, but still he didn't find the answer. A few minutes ago Gloria and I were talking, and I said I had hopes for people—that they were learning. But now that you mention mountain climbing, I am not so sure."

"What did Uncle Herman do to try to find out about mountain climbing?" Witherspoon asked. "Look in the encyclopedia?"

"Goodness no," Aunt Myrtle said. "He tried that in the early stages. Why, we spent hours in the Firestone Library, going up and down the stacks looking for books on mountain climbing. We went through dozens of volumes, but we never discovered the reason. That was why Herman decided to embark on that insane adventure. When he got curious nothing could stop him."

"What insane adventure?" Witherspoon asked. "What did he do?"

"Why he climbed the Matterhorn!" Aunt Myrtle said proudly. "And before you show your ignorance by asking where the Matterhorn is, I will tell you. It is a mountain in the Alps. A very big mountain, not the tallest mountain in Europe, but almost. And certainly the most difficult to climb. Herman was the first turtle ever to climb it. And I suppose the only one."

"Did he climb with some people?" Witherspoon asked.

"He certainly did not!" Aunt Myrtle said. "He did it entirely on his own. Now I want you to notice that I did not say that he was the first *living creature* to ever climb the Matterhorn. He did beat any *human* to the top, but we turtles are not immodest as humans are. You notice when you read a book how they put everything in terms of themselves. They say Columbus was the first to discover America. Or a few might say it was Leif Ericson or the Indians. Why hundreds of birds and turtles and fish and other animals discovered it long before man. People are extremely self-centered. You'll hear them make a remark such as, 'What good is a mosquito?' What they really mean is what good is it to them? Mosquitoes are lots of good to turtles. I find them very tasty."

"They're kind of bitter," Witherspoon said.

"When you're young, you always have a sweet tooth," Aunt Myrtle said. "When I was your age I loved chocolate."

I knew if she got off on the subject of food, she would never tell us about Uncle Herman's mountain climbing. Aunt Myrtle loves food and would almost as soon talk about it as eat it.

"Tell us about Uncle Herman's climb," I said.

"That's right. I was talking about Herman. Well, this was years ago—more than a hundred years ago as a matter of fact. They were fighting the Civil War here in the United States. Most of the students from Princeton went. Herman and I felt the war was unnecessary, and it depressed us. But it wasn't our affair, so we went off to Europe on a vacation. We were in France for a while, and then we went to Switzerland. We were up in some of those high alpine fields that are so beautiful, hunting for lingenberries, when Herman got the idea to climb the Matterhorn.

"People were climbing mountains all over. It had become sort of a craze. Herman and I could not figure it it out. No human had ever climbed the Matterhorn. As I mentioned earlier, very possibly some living creature had climbed it long before. Maybe a mountain goat, or for all I know, an alligator. Animals don't go around boasting, so such things are soon forgotten. Anyhow, while we were there, a mountain climber named Sir Edward Whymper was organizing an expedition to climb the Matterhorn and everyone was talking about it.

" 'What do you suppose is up on top of all these mountains that they go to such effort to get there?' Herman asked.

" 'I can't imagine,' I said.

" 'Maybe eagles fly up to the tops of mountains and lay golden eggs?' Herman suggested.

" 'I don't think so,' I said. 'We turtles know a little bit about eggs and certainly no turtle ever laid a golden one. And I've talked to geese, and they say that it is just nonsense about killing the goose that laid the golden egg.'

" 'Then maybe there are diamonds up there,' Herman said. 'Maybe the lightning strikes the top of the mountain and forms diamonds.'

" 'Highly unlikely,' I said. 'I heard a chemistry professor say once that diamonds were made of carbon. And where would any carbon come from way up on top of a snow-covered mountain? Besides if there are diamonds up there what difference would it make? We don't want any. Turtles gave up silly things like jewelry ages ago.'

" 'I don't want any diamonds and I don't want any gold,' Herman admitted. 'I just want to know why people climb mountains.'

"Herman was a true scholar. He liked knowledge for knowledge's sake. The more he heard about Sir Edward Whymper's expedition, the more interested he became. This was in the summer of 1864. One day he announced that he had decided to climb the Matterhorn. I did all I could to dissuade him, but it was no use. So I helped him catch bugs for several weeks so that he could store up food. I went with him to the snow line and said good-by. I stayed there in a beautiful upland meadow, surrounded by edelweiss. I love the perfume of edelweiss, and the blossoms aren't bad eating either. I stayed for several days watching, while Herman climbed farther and farther. Finally he was just a tiny spot on the snow, and at last he disappeared entirely. The nights were too cool to suit my taste so I went south into Italy. We had agreed to meet in Pompeii in six weeks. I visited around Italy, and exactly six weeks later I was in Pompeii. Herman did not appear. I waited and waited, almost three months, but there was no sign of Herman. Finally I decided I would never see him again —that he had died up there in the snows of the Matter-horn.

"I enjoyed Italy and the Italian turtles were very hospitable, but we didn't seem to speak the same language, so I stowed away on a ship and came back to America.

"The following year, 1865, Sir Edward Whymper climbed to the top of the Matterhorn. Even though everyone here was occupied by the Civil War, Sir Edward's climb was in all the papers. Four of his party fell to their death on the way down. It was very tragic.

"About six weeks after Sir Edward's great exploit, who should come walking along Nassau Street but Herman. I was overjoyed to see him. I should have known a little mountain like the Matterhorn would never be too much for Herman."

"Did he get to the top?" I asked.

"He certainly did," Aunt Myrtle replied. "At first he didn't want to talk about it, but gradually the truth began to come out. He had a horrible time."

"Why?" Witherspoon asked. "Did he fall in a crevasse?"

"No. His trouble was with the cold. As you know we turtles get very sleepy and slow when we get cold. Herman kept going slower and slower the higher he went and the colder he got. The cold didn't actually cause him to suffer, it just made him want to go into hibernation. It took sheer willpower to keep going at all. Each night when the sun went down, he would go off to sleep, and only if a warm sun came out the next day, would he wake up at all. He said he lost all track of time and may have slept for days at a time if the sun didn't shine. But Herman was determined and he kept on.

"He slipped once and went right over a sheer cliff. Fortunately he landed in soft snow at the bottom. He finally managed to dig his way out, although he got so cold that his toe nails got very brittle and half of them snapped off. But finally he clawed and burrowed his way out. He felt like giving up, he had fallen so far, but Herman was never a quitter. He started climbing again. Weeks passed and he kept plodding upward. Finally one night he arrived at the top. It was a beautiful clear night, and he said he could see for miles and miles. There were lights twinkling far below in the villages. All sorts of lights. That was the first time that he knew how much time had passed."

"How did he know?" Witherspoon asked.

"It was Christmas Eve," Aunt Myrtle said. "He saw all the lights on the trees. Well, after he had looked around for some time, he decided that even though the view was magnificent, no one would climb all that way just to look. He felt there must be something else. He went to sleep thinking that when the warm sun woke him in the morning he would look around the mountain-top and hunt for diamonds or rubies or whatever might be there.

"It began to snow during the night—a very heavy snow. Herman was covered by feet upon feet of snow. With neither the light nor the warm sun to wake him, he kept on sleeping. He slept all through the winter. It was late next summer, when some of the snow had melted, that he finally woke up. He looked down the mountain and there struggling toward the peak was Sir Edward Whymper and his party. Herman couldn't see anything of interest himself on the top, but he decided since he had already been so long, he might as well wait a while longer. Then he could see exactly what humans found when they got to the top. So he waited two more days until they arrived."

"And what was there?"

"Nothing!" Aunt Myrtle said. "Absolutely nothing! They planted a little flag on the peak, slapped each other on the back, told each other how great they were, they rested, and then they started down. They didn't even *hunt* for anything! The only reason they had climbed up all that distance was to be able to say they had reached the top."

"How peculiar," I said.

"That is expressing it very mildly," Aunt Myrtle said. "Herman was extremely disappointed and in a terrible rage. He reared up on his hind legs and danced around, he was so mad. Just then a gust of wind came blowing over the peak of the Matterhorn. It flipped Herman over on his back and sent him whirling down the icy face of a steep slope. You are not awake in the winter to see it, but I've shown you pictures of how children slide down snowy hills on sleds and toboggans. They

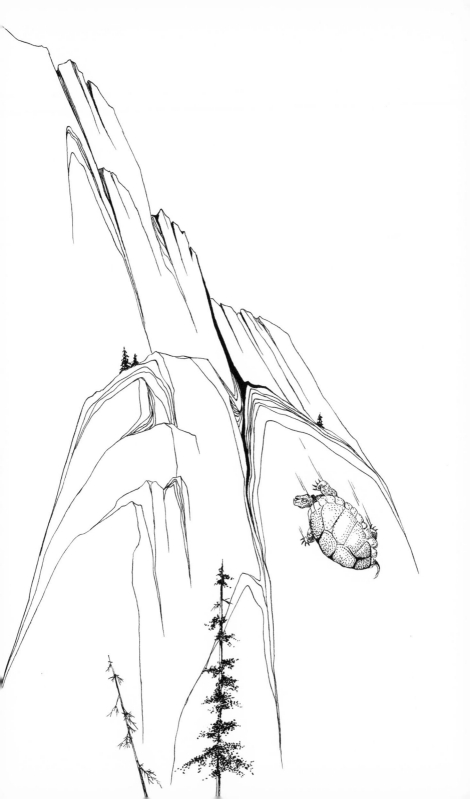

also slide down in big aluminum saucers, going round and round as they go. Well Herman was like that. The slopes on the Matterhorn are very, very steep, and he kept going faster and faster, round and round, spinning on his back. Finally he came to the edge of a great cliff, and he just went spinning off into space. He sailed out over icy crevices, huge fields of snow, and then over rocky slopes. He even went over the treetops as he got lower. In a matter of a few minutes he descended the Matterhorn, a distance that had taken him months to climb.

"He managed to get right side up finally, and by using his tail and his feet as rudders, he was able to guide himself a little. However, it was still largely luck that he finally glided into a tall fir tree. The soft needles broke his fall, and he landed safely on the ground. He was bruised a bit, and he was dizzy for a long time, but he was down. People are always talking about firsts, as I said. Herman was probably the first turtle to ever climb the Matterhorn, and I'm sure he made the fastest descent ever known. And I'm convinced there is still another first but I can't prove it."

"What's that?"

"Everyone was watching the Matterhorn every daylight minute and even most of the night, trying to keep track of Sir Edward Whymper's expedition. A number of people saw Herman flash across their telescopes. He looked like some strange, round dishlike flying object. There were all sorts of stories. I am positive he was the first flying saucer ever sighted. People have been seeing them ever since."

 *seven*

*A*unt Myrtle, Witherspoon, and I were taking a nap under a bush by Witherspoon Hall, when three students came walking across the campus. They stopped for a minute near us, waiting for a fourth student.

"Do you think this séance will be any fun?" one asked.

"I don't know. Sam says the one he went to was a blast. After a little while you get in the mood, and you find yourself believing that you really are in touch with spirits. Shivers run up and down your spine. Madam Weaver is good, and it's quite an honor to be invited. But don't go if you aren't interested."

"Oh, I'll go," the other student said. "Be sort of fun to meet a spook. I've met everything else in Princeton."

"What were they talking about?" Witherspoon asked after the students had walked on.

"A séance," Aunt Myrtle said.

"What's a séance?"

"It's a meeting where a lot of people get together in a half-dark room and hope that spirits will get in touch with them."

"What's a spirit?" Witherspoon asked.

"That's a ghost, silly," I said. Witherspoon can be very, very ignorant at times.

"I'm not sure what a ghost is," Witherspoon complained.

"Nobody else is either," Aunt Myrtle said. "We turtles are much more exact than people are. The English language can be very confusing. Many words mean almost the same thing. Most humans believe that when a person dies some part of him goes to another world. In a church this is called a soul. People who believe in séances call this a spirit or shade and believe it comes back and talks to people who are still alive. Other people believe spirits can be mean and mischievous. They hang around gloomy old houses and scare people in the middle of the night. Then they are usually called ghosts. Of all of them the ideas about ghosts are the silliest."

"Why?" I asked.

"Well, ghosts are supposed to wear big white sheets. Now, I ask you, why would any ghost that could come and go from this world to another bother running around in a silly, awkward bedsheet?"

"Why couldn't it wear a mink coat?" I asked.

"Exactly," Aunt Myrtle agreed. "Or to be even more sensible and attractive, a turtle shell. There would simply be no excuse for a ghost to be badly dressed."

"Tell us more about these séances," Witherspoon said.

"Some people call themselves mediums and claim they have special powers that allow them to get in touch with spirits."

"How, with a walkie-talkie?" Witherspoon asked.

"Nothing that modern," Aunt Myrtle said. "Spirits usually talk to people by rapping on tables or moving chairs around."

"That's pretty stupid," I said. "I'd think they could figure out better ways of talking than by pounding on a table."

"Maybe they're hungry," Witherspoon said. "Are they?"

"Don't ask me," Aunt Myrtle said. "I'm just telling you what some people believe. You have to remember that people aren't as intelligent as turtles, and they have lots of silly ideas. All I know is that at a séance, people sit around a big table, usually in a half-dark room, while one of them who says he or she has special powers, tries to persuade spirits to get in touch with them."

"Why?" Witherspoon asked. My kid brother can ask more questions.

"Oh, all sorts of reasons," Aunt Myrtle said. "Suppose Gloria here was run over by a big truck on Nassau Street. Being very fond of her, you might want to get in touch with her if you thought you could."

"Are there turtle ghosts?" Witherspoon asked.

"I've never heard of any," Aunt Myrtle said. "Anyhow, people want to get in touch with spirits for various reasons, and so they have séances. I think half the time they don't really believe spirits can come back, but it's fun to go to a séance and feel shivers run up and down your spine. Your uncle and I used to watch one regularly just for something to do. It was more fun than the movies."

"Where?" I asked.

"Over on Library Place," Aunt Myrtle said. "There was an elderly woman named Mrs. Asquith who believed in spirits and was always trying to get in touch with the spirit of her husband. They had the séances in a big room that had French windows opening onto a terrace. Some of these were always open in the summertime. Herman and I would stroll over there on Thursdays and have a picnic on the terrace. We hid beneath a big potted rubber tree and ate bugs while they had a séance inside. It was fun."

"What sort of things did they do?" Witherspoon asked.

"All sorts of nonsense. One night a woman insisted she wanted to get in touch with her Aunt Caroline. When the medium finally said that Caroline was the one thumping on the table, this woman asked for the recipe for the bread-and-butter pickles Caroline used to make. There was a horrible banging and the table tipped over. The medium said that Aunt Caroline was angry at being called all the way back from another world for a pickle recipe. That's why she tipped over the table. But that was nothing compared to the night that the ghost of Library Place actually put in an appearance."

"What was the ghost of Library Place?" I asked.

"You mean you've never heard of him?" Aunt Myrtle asked in amazement. "I sometimes wonder if you young people learn anything these days. You don't seem to know anything about local history. The ghost of Library Place is the most famous ghost in Princeton! Probably in New Jersey, for that matter."

"Who was it a ghost of?"

"Well, as a matter of fact, it was your Uncle Herman," Aunt Myrtle said proudly.

"You just said there weren't any turtle ghosts," Witherspoon said. He was very proud at having caught Aunt Myrtle in a mistake.

"There aren't," Aunt Myrtle said calmly. "If I weren't so constantly interrupted I would be understood much better. I was about to say that people *thought* Uncle Herman was a ghost. The whole thing has a sensible explanation. It was very exciting at the time though. I thought surely Herman would be killed."

"Tell us about it," I said.

"You know perfectly well you couldn't stop her from telling us about it," Witherspoon whispered to me.

"Whispering is bad manners," Aunt Myrtle said. "And if you don't care to listen, you can leave."

"Oh, I'll stay," Witherspoon said grumpily. He always pretends he doesn't think much of Aunt Myrtle's stories, but he enjoys them as much as I do.

"Well, as I said before, Herman and I often went over to Mrs. Asquith's on Library Place to listen to their séances. One day in late June Mrs. Asquith's granddaughter Annabelle came to spend several weeks. She was about ten or eleven with big blue eyes, long blonde hair, and the sweetest, most innocent face I have ever seen on a human being. She looked like an angel. But we soon discovered she wasn't. She could think of more crazy things to do in ten minutes than I could tell you in ten days. Library Place and the streets around it are a stodgy neighborhood, but she certainly brought it to life."

"What did she do?" Witherspoon wanted to know.

"Everything," Aunt Myrtle said. "That little girl had

imagination. A neighbor a few doors away had a small fishpond in her garden. It held a number of goldfish. Annabelle went down to the fish market and bought a huge fish. It was at least two feet long. Dead of course. She put it in that tiny goldfish pond and then waited for the woman to discover it. Another time she caught about a dozen butterflies. She slipped into the kitchen of a neighbor, who was a friend of Mrs. Asquith's, and put all the butterflies in one of the kitchen cabinets so they would fly out when the door was opened." Aunt Myrtle chuckled. "But the best trick was one she played on a boy named Simon who was visiting a few doors away. He deserved exactly what he got."

"Why? What did he do?" I asked.

"He was mean," Aunt Myrtle said. "He was about the same age as Annabelle but about twice her size. He was in the kicking stage that some boys go through. When he walked along he looked for things to kick. It didn't make much difference what—a stick, a pine cone, or a cat that walked by. One day he saw me just as I was about to crawl through the hedge into the Asquith property. He kicked me so hard that I was sore for a week. I went skidding along the sidewalk and almost into the gutter. That same day, a few hours later, he was passing by again. Annabelle was playing on the lawn with a big rubber ball. It was about the size of a volleyball. The ball got away from Annabelle and rolled out toward the street. Simon gave it a great kick, and it went rolling down the street for almost half a block. Before Annabelle could catch it, it rolled in front of a truck and was squashed. It was split wide open.

Simon thought it was funny, but Annabelle was furious. He picked on the wrong person. Inside of five minutes she was at work on a plan to get even."

"How?" I asked.

"She took the ball home and taped the split shut with two or three Band-aids, leaving a little hole. Then she filled the ball full of water and put it in her grandmother's freezer. The next morning she was ready when she saw Simon walking by. She ran and got her ball and let it roll out front. Then she yelled at him *not* to kick it. Naturally he did. He ran for the ball and kicked as hard as he could. It was a solid block of ice. I don't know whether he broke his toe or not, but he limped around for weeks. He stopped kicking things."

"I thought you were going to tell us how Uncle Herman got to be the ghost of Library Place," Witherspoon complained.

"I am," Aunt Myrtle said in a very annoyed voice. "I'm just telling you the background of what happened. This younger generation is so impatient. After you have lived for a few hundred years, you'll discover there is really no rush. Anyhow, Herman and I saw Annabelle now and again. One night she slipped out of her room, down the back stairs, and hid in the bushes near us. She listened and watched the whole séance. All the people inside seemed to be very pleased and impressed that evening. The medium said that they were making great progress and that next week they should be able to get in touch with several spirits they had been trying to reach for months."

"Was Annabelle scared?" I asked.

"She giggled the entire time," Aunt Myrtle said. "Not very loud, of course, because she was supposed to be in bed asleep.

"The next week we went over to the Asquith's in the late afternoon. There was some choice shrubbery that Herman liked and quite a few tasty bugs in the garden, so we often had dinner there. Annabelle was home alone when we arrived. Her grandmother had gone to do some shopping. Annabelle was very busy. Her room was right above the big parlor where they held the séances. She had made a ghost out of a bedsheet. She hung the sheet over a coat hanger, made two black blobs for eyes and another black blob for a mouth."

"Why does a ghost need a mouth if he talks by pounding on tables and things like that? He doesn't eat does he?"

"I suggest you find a ghost and ask it," Aunt Myrtle said. "All I know is that this was Annabelle's idea of a ghost, and it was as good as anyone's. She threaded a string through the sheet and attached it to the coat hanger. Then she lowered it from her window. She came downstairs to see if she was dangling it in the right spot, where it could be seen easily by the people in the room below. When she yanked on the string the ghost would jounce around. It didn't look very scary to me—just an old sheet with spots on it—but then it was broad daylight, and also we turtles aren't superstitious as people are. Annabelle seemed satisfied. She pulled her ghost back up, rolled it into a ball, and stuck it on the window sill behind the drapes that hung there.

"She came downstairs again and started across the yard. I don't know what she intended to do, but she spotted Herman. She picked him up and saw the initials on his shell. She was interested and went back upstairs where she had a lot of books. She got one out and thumbed through the pages to discover exactly what kind of turtle Herman was. The minute she put Herman down, he tried to get away and headed for the door. Annabelle was still hunting for a picture of a turtle like Herman when the Asquith cat came in. It was a big tiger cat named Wee Willie. Naturally, Wee Willie took a swipe at Herman. As you know we turtles don't worry much about cats. We can just close our shells and wait for a cat to get tired and go away. The most a cat can do is make a few scratches on our shells. But Annabelle was worried. She picked Herman up and put him up on top of the books on her bookshelf, where she thought he would be safe from the cat.

"Her grandmother came home, and Annabelle hurried downstairs to help carry in the groceries. She forgot all about Herman. I was still outside, as worried as could be. I had no idea what had become of him. For all I knew he might be in the kitchen being made into turtle soup. The only thing I could do was wait. That's what I did. I waited, and it got dark, and then I waited some more.

"About dinnertime a woman who lived a few blocks away appeared and said she had just learned that Annabelle was visiting. Her daughter was having a cookout and later a swimming party, and she thought Annabelle might like to come. Naturally she went. I guess she forgot about her ghost or figured she could use it another time. And she certainly forgot about poor Herman. Mrs. Asquith was happy to have Annabelle go off to a party. I think she felt a little silly about having séances in her house and hoped Annabelle wouldn't know anything about them.

"People began arriving about eight o'clock, and about nine when it was dark, the séance began. For a while nothing happened. The medium talked for a time, and then there was silence. There were a few creaks, and someone claimed to have felt something brush past his shoulder. Then there were some mysterious thumps, and the medium said the spirits were arriving. What she didn't know, and I didn't either at the time, was that poor Herman was moving around on the bookshelf and had slipped down behind the books. He was wedged on his side between the books and the wall. In kicking around and trying to get right side up he knocked some books off the shelf. When they fell on the floor, naturally they made thumps. The loudest thump was a big dictionary. That caused a lot of excitement downstairs.

"Herman wiggled and squirmed and finally reached the end of the bookshelf, knocking off a few more books in the process. The end of the shelf was directly over the window sill and not too far above it. Herman looked down and saw the rolled-up sheet that Annabelle had fixed up for her ghost. He thought it would cushion his fall, so he jumped off the end of the shelf. He landed on the bundled-up sheet all right, but he flopped over as he went off the edge of the shelf and landed on his back. Well, he kicked and he squirmed and tried to grab anything he could reach in order to get back right side up, and before he knew it, he was all wound up in the sheet.

"Wee Willie, that dumb cat of the Asquiths', came prowling along at this point, looking for trouble. The string that Annabelle had fixed up to dangle her ghost with was hanging down from the sheet, and of course, with Herman threshing around, it was wiggling. Cats are silly, you know. They love a wiggling string. I don't know what they think it is. Any half-witted turtle would know immediately that a string is only a string. But Wee Willie didn't. He started playing with it, and from what Herman figured out later, he must have been lying on his back having a wonderful time with the string. He got all wound up in it, and a loop got around his tail somehow. At that point Herman's wiggling caused the bundled-up sheet to fall off the window sill on the outside of the house. Herman was still all tangled up in it.

"As he felt himself falling, Herman clamped his jaws down on the only thing he could find—a piece of the sheet. The ghost unrolled in perfect position in front of the window of the room below. Herman was hanging desperately on to the back side of it. Everything hung there, all suspended by the string that was wound around the cat's tail. It must have hurt, because Wee Willie let out a horrible yowl. I've never heard a ghost, but a yowling cat is a good substitute. The people looked up from the séance, and there outside the win-

dow was a white ghost. It jumped around because Herman was holding on with his teeth and waving his feet around trying to get a foothold somewhere. And with each big wriggle of Herman's, the cat let out a yowl. It was slowly being pulled out of the window by its tail. Wee Willie was clawing desperately but losing. First I saw his tail, then his hind feet, and finally his head. He lost his last toehold, and the whole works came tumbling down almost in front of me.

"It was a great séance. Several people screamed, one woman fainted, and one man tried to hide under a sofa. Even the medium got scared and tried to run out of the room, but she tripped and fell and skinned her elbow. Annabelle would have loved it. It was too bad she wasn't there."

"Was Uncle Herman hurt?" I asked.

"He was sort of shaken up, but again he fell on the sheet, which cushioned his fall. He got all tangled up in the sheet for a minute. Wee Willie landed on his feet, of course, and took off for the bushes. He dragged the sheet and Herman with him for about fifteen feet. Then the string broke. I managed to get Herman untangled. I was certainly glad to see him. He was half smothered and all the excitement hadn't helped his nerves any. So while he rested for a few minutes, I dragged the sheet way in under the bushes and half buried it."

"What for?" Witherspoon asked.

"Well, Herman always believed in being nice to humans. He said all those people had wanted so badly to get in touch with a spirit, it would be mean not to let them think they had seen one. When they finally calmed down a little, they came outside with lights and looked around carefully. All they saw were two turtles, sound asleep. In about two days the story was all over town. We heard about fifteen different versions of the ghost of Library Place. You two are the first I've ever told the true story."

 *eight*

Witherspoon and I went by McCarter Theatre this morning. There was a big sign saying Fashion Show. Neither of us knew what a fashion show was. It wasn't until two thirty in the afternoon, so we didn't stay. Later, when we were having a caterpillar lunch under one of the oak trees near the University Store, Aunt Myrtle appeared. I asked her what a fashion show was.

"Usually some dress designer or a department store has the fashion show," Aunt Myrtle explained. "Attractive young women put on various dresses or coats and parade around so that people can see them. Most fashion shows are of women's clothes, but now and then they have shows of men's clothes."

"Why?" Witherspoon asked.

"Because women are more interested in clothes than men," Aunt Myrtle said.

"No, I meant why do they have fashion shows?"

"To sell clothes," Aunt Myrtle said. "The people in the audience look at the models wearing the clothes and think they would look just as nice. But the trouble is that a big fat woman isn't going to look thin just because she buys a dress that is worn by a slim model."

"Why is it so many people are unhappy with the way they look?" I asked.

"How do you know they're unhappy?" Witherspoon asked. "Maybe they think they're handsome walking around on two legs and with all that silly messy hair on their heads. We know they're silly-looking but they may not."

"I think Gloria is correct," Aunt Myrtle said. "People must think they are naturally ugly, or else why would they always be buying clothes? They are obviously trying to improve on the way they look without clothes. Now can you imagine a turtle trying to make or buy a long trailing dress." Aunt Myrtle stopped and giggled. "Can you picture me in a blue dress with sequins?"

"It would have to be shaped more like a dog blanket than a dress," Witherspoon said.

"I'll thank you to be a bit more respectful," Aunt Myrtle said huffily. "I do not resemble a dog in any way, thank goodness!"

"What did you call the young women who wear the dresses?" I asked.

"Models," Aunt Myrtle answered. "A model is also someone who poses for an artist who is painting a picture or making a statue. I used to do that kind of modeling."

"*You* did?" Witherspoon asked.

"*I* did," Aunt Myrtle said. "After all I am quite a handsome turtle, in case you didn't know. Artists have more perceptive eyes than young smart alecks like you. One artist in particular did. His name was Archibald Mullen, and he lived over on Prospect Avenue. He was a sculptor."

"What did you model? A half cantaloupe?" Witherspoon asked.

"You are most impertinent today," Aunt Myrtle said. "Have you ever thought of visiting your cousins in Arkansas?"

"I didn't know I had any," Witherspoon said.

We don't have any relatives in Arkansas as far as I know. Aunt Myrtle doesn't kid very often, so when she does, she usually fools Witherspoon.

"I modeled a turtle," Aunt Myrtle said proudly. "Mr. Mullen made a huge bronze statue of me. It's about five feet long."

"Where is it?" I asked.

"New York City," Aunt Myrtle said proudly. "They were putting up a big new office building on Fifth Avenue. There is a very fancy central court with a pool and fountain. And there in the place of honor is my statue. The company liked it so much that they use a picture of it on all their advertising."

"I'd like to see it," Witherspoon said. "It's too bad

they didn't put it here on the Princeton University campus."

"It would be a lot more interesting than some of the sculptures that are on the campus," I said. "I'm never certain when they put up a new piece of sculpture whether it is supposed to be a real sculpture or some sort of a joke the students are pulling."

"I agree," Aunt Myrtle said. "I think a statue of a turtle should look like a turtle and not like a polar bear. But your Uncle Herman liked modern art. He claimed you had to study it to appreciate it. He went to all the art lectures on the campus for years. That was how he met Mr. Mullen. We went over to Mr. Mullen's place one day to look at his garden. Herman had heard it was full of sculpture. It was. Just one little corner was left for Mrs. Mullen. She had planted a row of lettuce." Aunt Myrtle smacked her lips. "Herman enjoyed the sculpture, and I enjoyed the lettuce. While we were strolling around the garden, Mr. Mullen came out. He took one look at me and decided he would like me to pose for his statue. I think Herman was a trifle hurt that Mr. Mullen picked me."

"Did he do the statue all in one day?"

"Oh no, it took a long time. He made sketches, then a plaster model, and then a mold. There are a lot of steps in making a bronze statue. We went back any number of times. Mr. Mullen was very understanding. He didn't mind at all that I ate the lettuce. Mrs. Mullen wasn't so pleased though."

"Did your statue look like you?" I asked.

"Very much, that's why it was so good," Aunt Myrtle said modestly. "Not that Mr. Mullen didn't like abstract art. I think he was on an advisory committee that picked a number of the modern sculptures you see here and there on the campus. Your Uncle Herman thought Mr. Mullen had excellent taste—which of course he did now and then, such as when he picked me to model for him. But most of the statues he liked were awful—just plain awful. One was stolen one time, you know. Your Uncle Herman was the one who solved the crime."

"Uncle Herman solved a crime?" Witherspoon asked. "How?"

"You sound very doubtful," Aunt Myrtle said. "While your uncle's idea of what is beautiful in art may be silly, he was a great detective. In fact, I think he should be ranked with Sherlock Holmes and Maigret for the brilliance of his detective work. And he was a master at disguise."

"A turtle a master at disguise!" Witherspoon said. "That'll be the day!"

"Herman disguised himself as a cream can, as a floor lamp, and as a petunia planter," Aunt Myrtle said haughtily. "And all were very successful!"

"Aw, come on!" Witherspoon said. "How could he disguise himself as a floor lamp? That's the craziest thing I ever heard."

"Tell us how Uncle Herman solved the crime," I said.

"I wouldn't mind telling you," Aunt Myrtle said. "But this young wiseacre wouldn't believe me, so there is no point telling him. On your way, Witherspoon!"

"I happened to be here first," Witherspoon said, which was true.

"He'll behave," I promised. "Besides, he really wants to hear the story."

"Well, perhaps he'll learn something," Aunt Myrtle said. "And if he learned something every day for another thousand years or so, he might be almost as intelligent as his Uncle Herman."

Aunt Myrtle cleared her throat, dug herself a nice comfortable hole in the ground under a bush, cleared her throat again, and then began.

"Several years back there was a big rusty iron sculpture over near Nassau Street. It was a bunch of jagged pieces of iron, points, half circles, and triangular pieces, all welded together. I didn't understand it at all. I couldn't tell one end of it from another or the top from the bottom. Neither could the people who put it up, because they erected it upside down. The artist came to see it and was furious. They had to take it down and set it back up the other way to. It was called *Dialogue with an Egg Crate,* and the name didn't mean any more to me than the statue did. But Herman liked it. He said it gripped him right here." Aunt Myrtle put one paw over her heart.

"I used to spend a great deal of time down by that sculpture. One thing I'll say for it—it cast a nice shadow about three in the afternoon. And bugs seemed to like it, and I like bugs. But one day it disappeared. Just plain simply disappeared!"

"Where did it go?" Witherspoon asked.

"No one knew," Aunt Myrtle said. "It was very mysterious. Remember I said it was made of iron or steel. It was about ten feet tall, and it weighed several tons. Not just anyone could walk away with a statue like that. The college and the entire town were in an uproar. The Princeton police were so upset about it that they took five policemen off the parking ticket patrol to solve the crime. Some people said it was the finest thing that had ever happened to the Princeton police."

"Did they find the statue?" I asked.

"No one had even the faintest idea of how to find it," Aunt Myrtle said. "They had great consultations. Princeton University and the police got in touch with architects and art dealers and people all over the country. They sent out pictures of the stolen sculpture. As one detective said, 'You can't sell a sculpture that size to just anyone. Whoever bought it would need a park to put it in.'

"Several months passed and not one single clue was uncovered as to what had become of the sculpture. Famous detectives and art experts were called in from all over. They were baffled. Mr. Mullen felt particularly bad because he had recommended that the university buy it in the first place. It was largely because of Mr. Mullen that your Uncle Herman decided to take a hand.

"Herman had just read the complete works of A. Conan Doyle and he admired Sherlock Holmes very much. 'It should all be a matter of simple deduction,' he said. 'These detectives have not thought it through.' Herman ate a big meal and then went into deep meditation for four days. When he finally stirred he said, 'The trouble is that no one has been willing to admit that there are two sides to every question.'

" 'There is only one side to this question,' I reminded him. 'The statue is gone. The other side has it and it looks like it means to keep it.'

" 'There are two viewpoints to everything,' Herman said again. 'Now I think that sculpture was beautiful. What did you think it was?'

" 'A big piece of junk!' I said. 'And to judge from a lot of remarks I've heard, about half the people that have noticed that it's gone feel the same way.'

" 'Exactly,' Herman said. 'Two sides. But what have our great detectives concluded? All I've heard them mention is that whoever stole it considered it a work of art. Now many of us know it *is* art, but there are many, as you point out, who feel that it was a piece of junk.'

" 'I don't get the point,' I told him.

" 'Well, it could have been stolen as a work of art. The police have been in touch with art dealers. Or it could have been stolen as a piece of junk. Suppose some junk dealer took it. It could be in his junk yard. None of these great detectives have looked in the junk yards, have they?'

" 'That's a brilliant idea,' I told Herman. 'Because even if they didn't find the sculpture, they could find lots of other pieces of junk iron that would do just as well.'

"Herman ignored my remark. 'I will search the junk yards,' he announced.

" 'How are you going to search the junk yards?' I

asked. 'It would take years to hike to all of them in the surrounding twenty miles.'

" 'I will be carried to the junk yard,' Herman said. 'I have a plan. Whoever stole the sculpture thought it was a piece of junk, having no appreciation of true art. So I will disguise myself as a piece of junk, and the same junkman may pick me up.'

"I had no idea how he planned to do this, but Herman was resourceful. He located an old cream can, you know one of those big ten-gallon cans. He found it in a garage on Hamilton Avenue. One night we rolled that rusty old cream can all the way to Nassau Street. We set it in the same spot the statue had been. It was getting light as we finally got it in place. Herman climbed in, and I retreated to the bushes to watch.

"Nothing happened until about ten o'clock. Then a woman drove by in a big fancy car. She spotted the cream can immediately. She looked all around to see if anyone were looking and then quickly put the cream can in the trunk of her car. She drove off with poor Herman inside.

"It was four days before I saw Herman again. He came limping back to the campus, tired, dusty, and with sore feet from walking. That woman had taken him to her home near Lawrenceville. She took the cream can out of the car and carried it into a barn out back, which she used as a studio. Without looking inside she turned the can bottom up, trapping poor Herman. Then she proceeded to bang on it, scrape it, brush it with a wire brush, and rub it with sandpaper. Herman said the din almost drove him out of his mind. He suffered agonies. After two days she turned it on its side for some reason, and he was able to crawl off in a corner. She painted the cream can black and dull gold and decorated it with flowers. She called all her friends in and they all oohed and aahed over it. Finally she took it inside and set it beside her fireplace. Herman managed to get out of the studio and walked back to Princeton.

"Nothing could stop Herman once he had an idea. We found an old wooden churn and he crawled inside that. Some woman carried that off to make a lamp out of it. Next we located a heavy iron pot, and he hid in that. A woman carried that away and planted petunias in it. When she found Herman inside it, she threw him out in the garbage. He just missed being chewed into bits by one of those big garbage trucks. He was two weeks getting back from that adventure.

" 'The trouble is that the people of Princeton don't seem to be able to tell a piece of junk from something valuable,' Herman said. 'I'll have to find something no one can make into a lamp.'

"We finally located an old rusty lawnmower. We pushed and we pulled and we got it over to Nassau Street. Herman snuggled down among the blades. Well, no one wants an old hand-powered lawnmower. The whole day passed and nothing happened. Then the next morning a truck stopped and a man got out. He picked up the lawnmower and tossed it in the back of the truck. There was a sign on the truck door—Crazy Joe Schmo, Scrap Iron Dealer.

"Herman was gone only two days, and this time when I saw him coming down Nassau Street I knew half a block away that he had solved the case.

" 'It's there!' he said. 'And you would never believe what he has done to that beautiful work of art. He has hung hub caps, wheel rims, and all sorts of junk all over it. I was scarcely able to see it, he had it so covered.'

"My opinion was that it couldn't look any junkier than it had before, but I didn't say anything. I believe in being broad-minded. If Herman could admit that it looked like junk to someone like me, I ought to be willing to admit that it was art to him. 'What have you done about getting it back?' I asked.

" 'Nothing,' Herman said. 'It's too far and too heavy for me to try to get it here. This Crazy Joe character has a big truck with a hoist on it. He took it away in that, and that is the sensible way to bring it back.'

" 'But how will you get him to do it?'

" 'I figure I will let Mr. Mullen find the sculpture,' Herman said.

" 'But you won't get any credit at all for your brilliant detective work,' I objected.

" 'Turtles don't need public recognition,' Herman said. 'All I want is to recover a great work of art.'

"Herman really was anxious to get the sculpture back. He said he missed it very much—the campus looked bare. I missed it too but not in the same way. I don't know why the Art Committee or whatever it was called couldn't have put a beautiful statue of something like a big fat grub or a fly in that spot. But I was willing to help Herman get the old sculpture back if it would make him happy. We hiked over to Mr. Mullen's house and managed to sneak into his study. He had a battered old typewriter on his desk. It was a difficult job getting paper in the machine, and I had to type the message because Herman's feet were so big that he would hit several keys at once. Our message was very brief— 'Dialogue with an Egg Crate at Crazy Joe Schmos Junk Yard.' I made a couple of errors like leaving out the apostrophe in 'Schmos,' but then I don't type very much. We left the paper in the machine. A day or so later he found it."

"I suppose he got all the credit for solving the crime," Witherspoon said.

"No one got any credit. I was a little disappointed in the way Mr. Mullen handled the whole thing. He went out to the junk yard and found the statue. Then he came back and invited several others from the university, whoever the men were in charge of such matters, to his house for a big conference. It seems that Joe Schmo had seen this big hunk of rusty iron sitting on the grass near the road and thought it had been set out for the garbage man. Everybody else along Nassau Street had their garbage cans out. He knew the garbage man couldn't pick up that big thing, and he was in his truck with the hoist. So he picked it up, thinking he was doing everyone a favor. It happened quite early in the morning, and no one saw him do it. He was amazed to learn he had a valuable sculpture.

"The Art Committee didn't want to admit that one

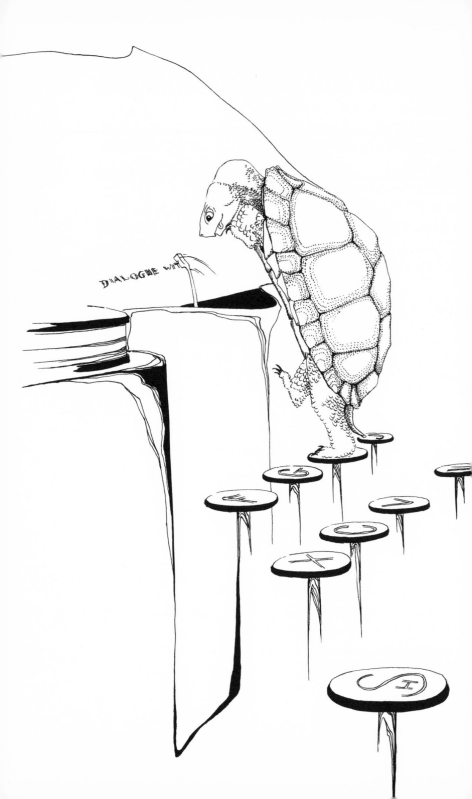

of its works of art had been mistaken for junk by a real junkman. They decided that they had to keep the story out of the newspapers. They agreed to forget the whole matter if Crazy Joe Schmo would bring the statue back in the middle of the night. That's the way it happened. One morning there was the sculpture again. To this day it is a complete mystery to the public. Herman, and the others who liked the sculpture, were happy again. As Herman said, 'You can do almost anything in this world if you don't worry about who gets the credit.' "

 *nine*

My brother Witherspoon can ask some of the silliest questions for a turtle, especially a turtle from such an intelligent family as ours. Yesterday, right out of a blue sky, he asked Aunt Myrtle why, if turtles were smarter than people, they had never invented an automobile.

"That's very simple," Aunt Myrtle said scornfully. "No turtle ever wanted a car."

"I do," Witherspoon said. "I'd like a nice little sports car. A Jaguar painted bright red would be about right."

"I beg your pardon," Aunt Myrtle said. "What I should have said is that no turtle in his right mind ever wanted a car."

"I do," said Witherspoon. "But I think I've changed my mind. I would like a bright blue Jaguar."

"My statement still stands," Aunt Myrtle said. "There are various reasons why humans invent such things as cars and turtles do not."

"Such as?" Witherspoon said.

"It ·is unbearably hot today," Aunt Myrtle said. "I need a rest. I walked all the way from Lake Carnegie up here to the library, and walking in the heat exhausts me. When I wake from my short nap, we will resume this argument, silly though it is."

She closed her eyes and a minute later was snoring softly. Witherspoon crept up quietly and looked closely at Aunt Myrtle. Then he came over and whispered in my ear. "Nap, my eye. She's pretending to sleep while she thinks up some answer for me!"

"She's not either!" I said. "Aunt Myrtle is probably the wisest turtle in the world, except possibly for Uncle Herman. I've never met him."

A gnat flew by Aunt Myrtle's nose. She opened one eye and when the gnat flew by again, she reached out and caught it in mid-air. "Now, let's see," she said. "Witherspoon, you were asking about why we turtles didn't invent something like an automobile. First, we don't need it. We're in no hurry to go anywhere. We're already here, and usually *here* is just as good a place to be as *there*, a fact that young people don't seem to comprehend. Second, we have a shell while people just have miserable paper-thin skins. We don't need a roof over us when we are traveling in the rain. People do. But even more important, we think things all the way through, humans do not. No doubt some turtle thought of an automobile long before Henry Ford or others like him had the faintest glimmer of an idea. Many turtles could have invented cars, but they didn't stop with thinking how nice it would be to have a contrivance that could zip around. They considered the long-range effects. First, for cars to be much good we would have to have roads. Turtles don't want to replace big stretches of beautiful grass with concrete. Concrete burns your feet, and it's certainly no place to hunt for bugs. Then we turtles considered all the noise hundreds and thousands and millions of cars would make, and of all the gasoline fumes and air pollution, and all the old car junk yards that there would be."

"I think maybe I'd rather have a good saddle horse than a sports car," Witherspoon said.

"That's a much better idea," Aunt Myrtle said. "Your Uncle Herman knew how to ride a horse. He rode a horse in the Kentucky Derby one time."

I would have liked to have heard about Uncle Herman riding in the Kentucky Derby, but Witherspoon was still worried about whether turtles were as smart as people. He certainly does get some wacky ideas.

"Why don't turtles have school like people do, if they are so smart?" he asked.

"I would think the answer to that question would be quite obvious even to someone as young as you are," Aunt Myrtle said. "Turtles don't need school. They are born smart and can take care of themselves almost from the minute they are hatched. People are born helpless and ignorant. Did you ever look at a tiny baby? It doesn't know anything and never would if it didn't go to school. Of course a few people are born brilliant and never have to go to school except for a short time. Take Thomas Alva Edison."

"Who is he?" Witherspoon asked. "And where should I take him?"

"Thomas Alva Edison was a genius who invented all sorts of things. You should know about him, he lived not far from here. He invented the phonograph, several inventions connected with the telegraph, movies, and lots of things. And he went to school only a few months."

"He invented electric lights too, didn't he?" I asked.

"Well, he is always given the credit," Aunt Myrtle said. "Actually, it was your Uncle Herman who gave him the bright idea."

"Why would Uncle Herman want to invent a light?" Witherspoon asked. "We can see all right in the dark."

"He didn't really invent it," Aunt Myrtle said. "He gave Edison the idea and Edison did the actual invent-ing. Herman's part was largely accidental, but then that's how many inventions came about."

"How did this one happen?" I asked.

"Your Uncle Herman and I were visiting some friends in Menlo Park, New Jersey. That whole area was quite rural and lovely back before the turn of the century. There were open fields with cows and big areas of woods. Now it's all houses, of course. Anyhow, in those days Thomas Edison had a laboratory in Menlo Park and was busy as can be, inventing all sorts of things. Most people know that he did a great deal with electricity—the telegraph and telephone, and phonograph, and motors. What not too many know is that he did quite a bit of work with plants too. One thing that interested him was the possibility of making some kind of rubber from plants that grow around here. He experimented with milkweed and all sorts of weeds. Some years later he did a lot of work for the United States trying to produce rubber from goldenrod. At the time Herman and I were visiting Menlo Park, he was experimenting with a variety of plants, particularly weeds that grow wild.

"Near where we visited there was a large field that for some reason or other wasn't being used. It had been planted to clover but had become a mixture of clover, ragweed, thistles, goldenrod, blackberries, and poison ivy. It was a lovely spot filled with huge mosquitos and other delicious bugs. We often went there for a picnic lunch. In addition to the bugs, there were delicious wild carrots and onions, and we could finish everything off by having some blackberries or elderberries for dessert.

"People left the field pretty much alone, because if they didn't get poison ivy they got scratched by the blackberry brambles. But one day we were surprised to find four men and a boy about fourteen working in the field. They had a number of glass jars, and they were busy cutting the stems of various weeds and trying to collect the sap. It turned out they were working for

Mr. Edison, collecting the sap from various plants in his early efforts to make rubber. They placed little glass jars all over the field and then left.

"Herman and I particularly liked that field because of the fireflies. At night the place was alive with them. They twinkled like a fireworks display. We often sat up for hours just to watch them. Fireflies aren't very tasty. Quite bitter, as a matter of fact. We never bothered them, and so turtles and fireflies have always been very friendly.

"Later in that same day the boy came back with a big basket-like tray and collected the glass jars. It was growing dark, and he missed several. As it got dark a little girl who lived nearby wandered into the edge of the field and found one of the jars. Each one had its own little black lid, which was attached to the jar with a wire. She put the lid on the jar and began collecting fireflies and stuffing them inside. Fireflies were everywhere, so it didn't take her long to catch half a jar full. Then in the half dark she scratched her nose on a huge blackberry bramble. She dropped the jar and ran home, crying her head off and holding her hand to her nose, which was bleeding like crazy.

"Herman ambled over to look at the jar. There were all those poor fireflies penned up inside with the air growing short. Herman set the jar upright and began working on the lid. He had it loosened so that at least they could get a bit of air, when back came the boy. He had counted the jars in Mr. Edison's laboratory, and he was three short. Each one was numbered so he knew about where they were. He located the other two easily enough but had trouble finding the third because the little girl had moved it. I warned Herman that the boy was getting near but he wanted to get the lid off. Suddenly the boy spotted the jar, and he did exactly what I expected he would do. He not only picked up the jar but Herman too. I don't know why it is, children can't resist taking turtles home with them. He stuck the glass jar and Herman into his basket and off he went.

"When he got to Mr. Edison's laboratory he placed the basket on the work counter and hurried home to dinner, forgetting all about poor Herman. There Herman was, stranded in a basket in a strange building. He managed to climb up and peek over the edge of the basket. Thomas Edison was fast asleep on a couch a few feet away. Edison was famous for working all sorts of hours. He took short naps when he felt tired and then went right on working whether it was night or day.

"Naturally Herman wanted to get out of the basket and the building. Edison looked like a kind man, and Herman couldn't think of any reason why a famous inventor would want a box turtle—or a jar full of fireflies either for that matter. He felt if he could only attract Edison's attention, both he and the fireflies would be set free. He tried climbing up the edge of the basket, but each time he slipped back. Finally he decided to push one of the jars over the edge with his nose. He picked the one with the fireflies. He thought when it hit the floor it would break. That would let the fireflies loose and wake Edison at the same time. He managed it, but when the jar hit the floor it didn't break as Herman expected. The noise did wake Mr. Edison though. He was a very light sleeper.

"He sat up in bed and looked around to see what had startled him. Then he saw this jar on the floor. All the fireflies were shaken up and excited by the fall, and they were flashing their tail lights like mad. Edison sat on the edge of his couch in that dark laboratory and stared at that jar.

" 'That's it!' he said finally. 'A glowing hot wire inside a glass jar. I'll call it a light bulb!'

"He was very excited. He got up, picked up the jar and glanced at the basket. I suppose he wondered what a jar of fireflies was doing in his laboratory and why it had fallen off the counter. Then he saw Herman.

" 'Well, it looks like young Jimmy has been collecting other things than milkweed sap,' he said. 'But between you, you've given me a great idea.'

"He took Herman and the jar of fireflies to the door and let them go. Then he went back to his worktable and began inventing the electric light bulb."

 *ten*

Witherspoon disappeared about a week ago and didn't appear until this morning. Aunt Myrtle and I were quite worried about him. We wondered if some big truck had run over him and squashed him or if some person had picked him up and had taken him away. People have a habit of doing that. They seem to think a turtle should be happy any place, so they take them home and put them in their flower garden or some place like that. They never think that a turtle might be homesick. I'm used to the Princeton University campus and I like it there. I wouldn't be happy at some place like Yale or Harvard, for example. The education may be just as good, but there's a very poor quality of bugs, I understand.

Witherspoon showed up this morning perfectly all right. I felt very relieved, and I know Aunt Myrtle did too.

"Where have you been?" Aunt Myrtle asked.

"I took a walk in the country," Witherspoon said.

"It must have been quite a walk."

"It was," Witherspoon said. "Turtles don't walk fast you know, and I was in no hurry."

"I know turtles don't walk very fast," Aunt Myrtle said drily. "I happen to have been one for years and years. Just where did you go on this walk in the country?"

"Out by the Princeton Airport," Witherspoon said.

"That shouldn't have taken a week, even at a slow amble," Aunt Myrtle said. "What happened?"

"Well, I got lost," Witherspoon admitted.

"You got lost! Turtles have the finest sense of direction in the world. How could you get lost?"

"A great big bird flew over and scared me, so I forgot which way I was going," Witherspoon said. "I headed in the wrong direction but before I realized it, I had gone miles."

"Turtles have nothing to fear from birds," Aunt Myrtle said scornfully. "At least not turtles your size. Not even a big owl or hawk tries to attack a turtle. You just close your shell, and you're perfectly safe. Once in a while a bird will try to pick up a turtle, the way a sea gull does a clam, but that's pretty difficult with box turtles like us. Our backs are so rounded they can't get hold of us."

"I know," Witherspoon said. "I've been told all that. But this was the biggest bird in the world. It could have picked up a giant sea turtle."

"Was it as big as a turkey?" I asked.

"Lots bigger."

"As big as an ostrich?" I asked.

"Much bigger than that," Witherspoon said. "I told you it was the biggest bird in the world."

"Was it longer than an automobile?" Aunt Myrtle asked.

"Lots longer, and it had long narrow wings."

"I see," said Aunt Myrtle. "Did it make any noise?"

"Just a *whoosh* as it went over."

"And you were out near the airport?"

"Yes."

"That wasn't a bird at all, silly," Aunt Myrtle said. "It was a glider."

"What's a glider?" Witherspoon asked.

"It's sort of a lightweight airplane without any motor," Aunt Myrtle explained. "It just glides through the air the way a hawk or a sea gull does when it locks its wings and glides around in great circles. Usually a glider glides downward toward the earth, but if an air current catches it, it can glide up for a while. A man sits in the pilot's seat and steers it this way and that."

"If it's a glider with a man in it but no motor, how does it get up in the air in the first place?" Witherspoon asked. "Does he pedal it like a bicycle?"

"No. Gliders can take off from the ground if they are towed by something like an automobile and there is a wind. But most of the time they are towed way up in the air by a small airplane. Then when they are high enough, they are cast loose and they glide back to earth."

"That sounds like fun," I said. "Gliding through the air with no sound except the wind. Like being a bird."

"I imagine it *is* fun," Aunt Myrtle said. "Sometimes I've regretted that we turtles didn't grow wings millions of years back. But then we have great beauty, and marvelous brains, and our own shell house to live in. I guess we can't have everything."

"Did Uncle Herman ever go up in a glider?" Witherspoon asked.

"No, he always wanted to. The closest he came was a balloon ascension."

"What's a balloon ascension?" Witherspoon asked.

"It's going up in a balloon."

"How could anyone get inside a balloon?" Witherspoon asked. "The neck is too small."

"Not an ordinary balloon like the ones children have," Aunt Myrtle said. "These are enormous big things, as big as a small house. You don't actually get inside the balloon. There is a net around it, and a sort of basket hangs from this. People get in the basket, and the balloon takes them way up in the air."

"How do they get down?" I asked.

"And how can you make the balloon go where you want it to go?" Witherspoon added.

"When Herman was making his balloon ascents, I learned quite a bit about balloons," Aunt Myrtle said. "In fact I might be called an expert. I doubt if any turtle in the United States knows as much as I do about balloons. Or any Princeton undergraduate for that matter. And since you seem sadly ignorant about both gliders and balloons, I might as well start at the beginning. Balloons are the earliest forms of aircraft, and men thought up schemes for them in the thirteenth century. The first successful ones were invented by the Montgolfiers in France. In 1783 they took a huge linen bag and filled it with hot air. Hot air is lighter than cool air, and the balloon went up and drifted almost a mile before it came down."

"Hot air!" Witherspoon whispered to me. "Balloons

run on hot air! That's why she knows so much about them."

"What did you say?" Aunt Myrtle asked suspiciously.

"I said I didn't know balloons operated on hot air," Witherspoon said, looking as innocent as a newly hatched turtle.

"Hmm," said Aunt Myrtle doubtfully. "Anyhow, hot air was used for some of the early balloons. But hot air cools off, and the balloon comes down. So they soon began using gases like hydrogen or helium, which are much lighter than air. The gas bag can be made from silk or plastic or rubber-coated fabric. The car that hangs down below the balloon is called a gondola. It is usually filled with sandbags."

"What for?" Witherspoon asked. "Why would anyone want to go for a ride with a sandbag? Sand gets inside your shell and hurts."

"If you will just remain quiet for a minute or two, I will explain," Aunt Myrtle said. "The balloon is filled with light gas, and it rises through the heavier air, carrying the gondola, the passengers, and the sandbags with it. If the balloon goes too high, the operator can pull on a rope and open a valve to let some of the gas out. If the balloon starts to settle, one of the sandbags can be thrown over the side, making the gondola lighter, and the balloon will rise."

"Wow!" Witherspoon said. "That would hurt."

"What would hurt?" Aunt Myrtle asked sharply.

"To be walking along minding your own business and be hit on the head by a sandbag."

"I daresay it would," Aunt Myrtle said. "But I suppose the man looks before he throws the sandbag over the side."

"What about at night?"

"Quit quibbling about details," Aunt Myrtle said. "To get on with my story, your Uncle Herman got to know a man named Ludwig Fudge who was a great balloonist."

"Ludwig Fudge," Witherspoon said. "Imagine having a name like that!"

"No one used it," Aunt Myrtle said. "Everyone called him Nutty Fudge because he was always experimenting with balloons. He lived on the road to Hopewell. Your Uncle Herman became very interested in what was going on out at Nutty Fudge's little farm, and he went out quite often. One day when Fudge wasn't looking, Herman climbed in the gondola. Fudge came out and took off without noticing that Herman was a stowaway. When they were way up in the air he discovered Herman. It was quite a long flight, and he was glad to have company. After that he often took Herman up with him.

"Late in the summer there was a great balloon race out in Ohio. It was the time of year when they expected the winds to blow eastward, and so Mr. Fudge felt he would be heading back toward New Jersey."

"So it's the wind that decides what direction you go?" Witherspoon said.

"Largely," Aunt Myrtle said. "You can make your balloon go up or down, as I just explained, but you have to go where the wind takes you. That's why they usually hold balloon races where there is land all around, Ohio for example. No one would care to be blown out to sea. But to get back to my story, Nutty Fudge packed up his balloon and went to Ohio. He took Herman with him. The race aroused a lot of interest. It was written up in the papers and was on TV. The balloons were painted all sorts of bright colors. Mr. Fudge painted his to look like a huge piece of chocolate candy with a pecan on top.

"The take-off was a gala affair. All the brightly painted balloons were tugging at their ropes in a huge field. Thousands of people came to watch. A band played and the governor of Ohio made a speech. Finally all the balloons were cut loose, and they sailed up into the air while everyone cheered. Nutty Fudge let his balloon go higher than any of the others right at the start. He threw over an extra number of sandbags."

"He might have hit the governor," Witherspoon said.

"I doubt it," Aunt Myrtle said. "I think the governor had quit talking and had gone home by this time. Well, Fudge's balloon caught a high air current and began heading due east. All the others, which were lower, were blown to the southeast. Soon Mr. Fudge and Herman were alone in the sky. All the others were out of sight. Night came and still they headed eastward. Unfortunately the air was very cold. I think there was a cold air mass coming down out of Canada as they say in the weather reports. Herman got very sleepy, as we turtles always do when it's cold. Mr. Fudge put on his jacket and wrapped a blanket around himself. He had some hot coffee and a liverwurst sandwich, part of which he gave Herman.

"It got cloudy and the stars disappeared. After a while they had no idea what direction they were headed in. There wasn't much else to do, so they went to sleep. Herman was the first to wake up the next morning. He climbed up on the top of the sandbags and peeked over the edge of the gondola. What he saw startled and alarmed him. They were just barely skimming over the treetops, and the trees were stunted ones at that. Herman jumped down and gave a nudge to Mr. Fudge."

"Say, you're a poet!" I said.

"Well, yes I am, now that you mention it," Aunt Myrtle said modestly. "A very fine poet, as a matter of fact. Did I ever tell you about the time Herman and I won the poetry contest? You had to submit an outstanding limerick to even enter the contest."

"What's a limerick?" I asked.

"Hey, finish the story you started," Witherspoon objected.

"A limerick is a special five-line verse," Aunt Myrtle said. "Just by chance I remember ours.

> *There was a young turtle named Grover*
> *Who was covered with rubies all over.*
> *Said Grover, "I declare,*
> *I'd much rather wear*
> *A hand-knit turtle-necked pullover."*

"Why I think that's marvelous!" I said.

"So did the judges," Aunt Myrtle said.

"I think it's terrible," Witherspoon said. "It stinks. No turtle would wear rubies or a pullover sweater."

"Some people have no culture—no appreciation of the finer things," Aunt Myrtle said with a sigh. "A limerick is supposed to be nonsense."

"That one certainly is," Witherspoon said. "How about finishing your story?"

"I thought you really didn't want to listen," Aunt Myrtle said with a sniff. "Let's see, where was I?

"Oh, yes, there they were in the dawn's early light, drifting along over the treetops in danger of being wrecked any minute. What had happened was that during the night the gas in the balloon had contracted and the balloon wasn't quite so buoyant. Also they were over mountains. So the balloon had gone down, and the land had come up and they were in danger of meeting any minute. Mr. Fudge immediately threw over his three remaining sandbags and the balloon rose slightly. The wind was still blowing, and they went skimming along. Although it was sort of misty or hazy, they could see where the sun was and they were still heading eastward.

" 'I think we are over the Pocono Mountains in eastern Pennsylvania,' Mr. Fudge said. 'We've come a long, long way. If we keep on at this rate we'll be over New Jersey soon.'

"Just then Herman saw something ahead that made his blood run cold. And since we turtles are naturally cold-blooded animals you can imagine it was something very serious. He nudged Mr. Fudge again and pointed with one claw."

Aunt Myrtle paused and shook her head sadly. Witherspoon got a stubborn look on his face. He knew she wanted him to ask what Herman had seen, and he wasn't going to. Finally I did.

"He saw a huge high-voltage electric line," Aunt Myrtle said. "Fifty-five thousand volts or some such terrible thing! And they were headed straight for it. It was quite a bit higher than the trees. They both knew if they hit the wires they would be electrocuted instantly. No one would know what happened. Some light bulb some place would give a slight flicker, and that would be all that marked the end of two of the world's greatest balloonists."

"Wouldn't the repairmen know when they found that big balloon hanging from the wires?" Witherspoon asked.

"Well, yes. I suppose they would," Aunt Myrtle said. "But to get on with my story, Mr. Fudge threw over his lunch basket, his bottle of coffee, his jug of water, and finally his blanket and jacket. The balloon rose slightly, and for a few minutes it looked as though they might sail over the wires. Then when they were only a few feet away, they realized they would be a few inches too low. It was too late to do the only other thing Mr. Fudge might have done—let gas out of the bag and crash into the trees. Herman was poised on the rim of the gondola. He was always a quick thinker. He realized that only he could save the balloon and Mr. Fudge. It was a great and noble decision."

Aunt Myrtle paused again, and this time Witherspoon couldn't stand the suspense.

"What did he do?" he screamed.

"You needn't shout," Aunt Myrtle said with a pleased smile. "Herman jumped over the side. He was quite a heavy turtle, and the difference of his weight was enough. The balloon rose slightly and cleared the wires by less than an inch."

"What became of poor Uncle Herman?" I asked.

"Well, Herman was practical as well as noble," Aunt Myrtle said. "He had noticed that there was a pond right beneath them. He figured he had just as good a chance of living through a long dive into the water as he would if he hit the electric wires. He closed his shell tightly on the way down and hit the water on his back. A turtle shell is a wonderful protection. He went down and down through the water and was still moving with some speed when he hit soft mud. It took him a while to get up out of that and to the edge of the pond. But he was unhurt."

"What happened to Mr. Fudge?" Witherspoon asked.

"He finally came down just west of Hoboken," Aunt Myrtle said. "He won the race. He got a gold medal and a prize of five hundred dollars. But he felt so bad about Herman sacrificing his life that he gave up ballooning forever. He couldn't come out and tell the newspapers that he owed his life to a turtle. They wouldn't have believed him. He simply said he had lost a dear friend. But of course Herman and I knew."

"Why didn't Uncle Herman go see him so he would know Herman had been saved?" I asked.

"Because Mr. Fudge moved away before Herman got back," Aunt Myrtle said. "It's a long hike from the Poconos to Princeton. Mr. Fudge went to California, where I think he went into the candy business. With his name, and being so famous, it was a sensible thing to do."

 *eleven*

Witherspoon and I went to a movie today at the Garden Theatre. It was all about otters and how they play in the water. Witherspoon and I usually go to matinees because there isn't such a rush. There is less danger of being stepped on by some big clumsy person. We don't have to have tickets. We crawl right past the ticket taker. He never notices us. Usually we get the best seats in the house, right in the front row.

On our way back we had to wait a long time to get across Nassau Street because there was a lot of traffic. We met Aunt Myrtle in the middle of the lawn in between the Firestone Library and Nassau Street.

"I wish I'd known what the movie was, I'd have gone with you," Aunt Myrtle said. "I very seldom go because movies are usually about people, and people can be so tiresome."

"Why don't they make more movies about animals?" Witherspoon asked.

"I guess because very few animals care to be actors," Aunt Myrtle said. "Especially wild animals. There are quite a few movies with parts for domesticated animals."

"What is a domesticated animal?" Witherspoon wanted to know. I didn't know either so I was glad that he asked.

"There is an entire library right behind us," Aunt Myrtle said. "It's filled with dictionaries and encyclopedias and reference books of all kinds. You should go look up the answers to questions like that."

"I can't reach the dictionaries," Witherspoon said. "They're way up on a high shelf. I'd hate to be a midget student at Princeton."

"True," Aunt Myrtle said judiciously. "The library does not seem to be designed with turtles in mind. But then that's natural. Turtles know so much they don't need to look up most things. At least some of us don't."

"Okay, if you know so much, tell me what a domesticated animal is," Witherspoon said.

"When man takes an animal and keeps it in captivity for generation after generation, it finally becomes used to that way of life. It becomes dependent upon man for its food and shelter. It is then said to be domesticated. Take cows, for example. There were once wild cows, and there may still be some in a few parts of the world. But most cows would starve to death if man didn't take care of them, in the winter at least. There are dozens of domesticated animals—horses, sheep, pigs, chickens, ducks, dogs, cats, guinea pigs, and oodles and oodles of others."

"People certainly must like to work, feeding so many animals," I said.

"They're out of their minds," Aunt Myrtle said. "Have you noticed that woman who walks down Nassau Street every day with that fat dachshund? She has to carry it across the street, and she spends half her time combing and brushing it."

"The dog has domesticated her," Witherspoon said.

"You may be right," Aunt Myrtle said, laughing. I didn't think it was such a funny remark.

"We're not domesticated animals are we?" Witherspoon asked.

"Most certainly not!" Aunt Myrtle said. "In the first place we are not ordinary animals. We are reptiles, which is a special category and the nicest. Second, we are too independent to ever depend upon man. And finally, to domesticate anything, man must have more sense than it does. Obviously that is not the case with turtles."

"I wouldn't like being penned up and being told what to do," Witherspoon said. "Domesticated animals must be pretty stupid."

"Not necessarily," Aunt Myrtle said. "We knew a little donkey named Gus some years back. He was quite intelligent. He enjoyed acting, oddly enough. He was in a number of productions at McCarter Theatre. He'd probably still be on the stage if it hadn't been for Herman."

"Why? What did Uncle Herman do?" I asked.

"I'm afraid he ruined Gus's acting career," Aunt Myrtle said sadly. "He didn't mean to. It was all an accident."

Witherspoon must have been feeling very polite. "Tell us about it," he said.

"Well, Gus was a little Sardinian donkey. He lived over toward Hopewell, as I recall. He got his first role on the stage in a play at Christmastime—about the birth of Jesus. Gus played the part of a donkey."

"What do you mean 'played the part of a donkey'?" Witherspoon asked. "He was a donkey, wasn't he?"

"I just said he was," Aunt Myrtle said indignantly. "He was a donkey, and in this play he played the part of a donkey. After all he might have played the part of a big rabbit. He was very small and had long ears."

"Did he ever play the part of a rabbit?" Witherspoon asked.

"No, I don't think so," Aunt Myrtle said. "He tried out for the part one time in a play about Peter Rabbit, but his voice was all wrong. Gus had a very loud and mournful bray. It was sort of a cross between a damaged pipe organ and a rusty door hinge. Anyhow, his first role was that of a donkey in a stable in Bethlehem. He did very well in the part, and all the critics said he was a fine actor. A few months later they put on a play about a pioneer family that lived in the barn with the animals for several years until the man finally built a separate log cabin. They didn't want to put great big horses and cows on the stage, so they had one sheep and Gus. It was a nice part. All Gus had to do was eat hay and look at the audience now and then. And looking at the audience at a play can be more fun than the play itself. In the middle of the second act on opening night, the woman on stage said, 'I think I hear music.' Just then Gus decided to bray. The audience loved it, and everyone clapped for five minutes. Gus was a real ham actor, and he decided he would do the same thing every performance. The trouble was that he was hard of hearing, and so he wasn't sure just when to bray. He and Herman were good friends, so he asked Herman to help him out. Lots of actors have prompters, you know. Herman went backstage each night for the two weeks that the play ran. At the right time, he nipped Gus on the heel. Gus would then bray. It worked perfectly, and Gus became famous overnight. The drama critics said he was the greatest actor to appear since Greta Garbo or Mickey Mouse.

"Next Gus had a few minor parts where he walked across the stage or something, and then he got a very important role in a musical comedy. It opened with a big outdoor western scene, with a campfire and bushes growing nearby, and a mountain painted in the background. Gus was a prospector's donkey and was tied to a little tree near the campfire. The prospector was joined at his campfire by some cowboys and cowgirls. They sang songs or danced during most of the first act. Gus thought it would be a good idea if he brayed at the right moment. He didn't know when that would be so he asked Herman for advice. Herman agreed to help him out as he had before, by nipping him on the heel.

"On opening night, Herman arrived early. Gus was already tied on the stage, nibbling a few wisps of hay. Herman went up to join him. There were rocks and logs scattered around, so a turtle just looked like another stage prop and no one noticed Herman at all. Gus and Herman talked for a few minutes, and then Herman wandered around the stage a bit to look things over. He was near the campfire when the stage director came out for a final inspection. A big round wastepaper basket had been turned upside down and painted to look like a tree stump. One of the singing cowboys was to sit on it while he played his guitar. The director picked this up and put it down again in what he thought was a better spot. That spot happened to be right on top of poor Herman.

"If the basket had been completely over Herman, it would not have been so bad. It would have been dark under it, but eventually I suppose someone would have picked it up again and Herman would have escaped. The trouble was that the edge of the rim was right across Herman's neck. It was a heavy metal wastepaper basket and it hurt. He tried to pull his head back into his shell but the edge of the basket caught against the back of his head. The worst part was that he knew he was headed for real trouble. He could feel death staring him in his lovely wrinkled face." Aunt Myrtle stopped and shook her head. "That is not a very good way to say it. He could feel death pressing down on his beautiful wrinkled neck."

"Why?" Witherspoon asked. "A wastepaper basket isn't all that heavy."

"That is true," Aunt Myrtle admitted. "But your Uncle Herman was a very observant turtle. He had been to one rehearsal, and he remembered that the singing cowboy who had sat on that stump was a hefty young man with a big fat posterior. When he sat down on the wastepaper basket, it would cut off Herman's head like a guillotine."

"What is a guillotine?" Witherspoon asked.

"It's a big machine with a heavy knife that can be dropped. They use it in France to chop off the heads of criminals, and now and then kings and queens. Herman had no intention of losing his head over a silly play. He hunched his shoulders, he tried to rear up on his hind legs, he shook his head—anything to get the basket off his neck. Nothing worked. Finally he decided the only thing to do was to get over near Gus and have Gus kick the basket off. He started crawling, dragging that big basket along with him.

"At this point the curtain rose, and the actors began strolling onto the stage. First came the prospector, then two cowboys, then several cowgirls, and finally this big fat guitar-strumming man who threatened to snuff out poor Herman's life. I was watching from the balcony, shivering with fright. Herman was having an awful time. The stage floor had been waxed, and he couldn't make much progress with that weight on him. Fortunately the guitar player wanted to strut, and he walked back and forth several times in front of the fire. Then he sat down where the tree-stump-wastepaper basket had been a few seconds earlier. It wasn't there any more. Herman had put on a desperate burst of speed. The guitar player landed with an awful thump. He was well padded and he wasn't hurt, but he dropped his guitar and it was damaged. Two strings were broken, and I don't know what else. They had to pull the curtain until they could get another guitar.

"Everyone was in a dither, and they didn't notice that the tree stump kept moving closer and closer to Gus. No one had thought to look for the missing stump when they opened the curtain a second time. The guitar player came on as before, and when he got ready to sit down there was no place to sit except on a papier-mâché boulder. It sagged under his weight a little but held. Then he started to sing. At this point Herman arrived at Gus's heels. As I said, Gus was hard of hearing. Herman tried, but he wasn't able to get his attention by hissing. So he bit him.

"The cowboy had sung about two lines, when Gus's mournful bray drowned him out. The cowboy faltered but kept on. Herman bit Gus again, and this time Gus brayed even louder. The audience howled. The cowboy stopped and said something to someone off stage. Then he started all over. So did Herman and so did Gus. Gus liked all the applause and laughing, so this time he really

134

filled the hall. The walls vibrated, he brayed so loud. One of the cowgirls jumped to her feet and started toward Gus. Gus finally looked back and saw what a terrible fix Herman was in. Gus was a true friend, and he thought quickly. He kicked out with both hind feet. The wastepaper basket went sailing through the air and hit the girl in the stomach just as she rounded the campfire. She fell backward right on top of the fire. It wasn't a real fire, but there must have been some pointed sticks in it or maybe she sat down on one of the light bulbs that made the fire glow. Anyhow, she let out a scream and rushed off stage. They had to pull the curtain again."

Aunt Myrtle sighed. "That was the end of Gus's acting career. It was also about the end of the play. It only ran three nights. It was all very unfair. The reviews all said that Gus was more on key than the guitar player, and he certainly was better-looking. Gus told Herman later that he really didn't mind. He was getting bored with the stage. About the only time he ever makes a public appearance these days is at Reunion, when he marches in the parade with all the Princeton grads."

Witherspoon was silent for a long time, which is very unusual. Aunt Myrtle finally asked him what was wrong.

"I was thinking about Herman," Witherspoon said. "Since he's so famous why hasn't anyone written a biography about him?"

"I am certain someone will someday," Aunt Myrtle said proudly. "Especially since he will be even more

famous when he returns from this last great adventure."

"Returns from what last great adventure?" I asked. "Isn't he dead?"

"Dead! Whatever gave you that idea? Herman is very much alive, I hope."

"Then where is he?" Witherspoon demanded. "I've never seen him. Gloria has never seen him. Nobody I know has seen him."

"He left on a mission several years back," Aunt Myrtle said, almost in a whisper.

"What kind of mission?" Witherspoon wanted to know.

Aunt Myrtle looked around carefully. Then she led us over to a spot beside the foundation of one of the buildings. We hid under a big shrub where it was very private and no one could come near without being seen.

"I was sworn to secrecy by Herman," she whispered. "You see if word got out it might get some people into serious trouble. Herman left Princeton in great secrecy, in the middle of the night in fact. You two are the first I've told this secret. He went to Florida."

"What's so secret about that?" Witherspoon asked.

"He went to Cape Kennedy," Aunt Myrtle said mysteriously.

"Where they launch the rockets?" I asked.

"Exactly. His original plan was to stow away on Apollo 16 but something went wrong. He sent me a message shortly afterward that he had missed it. However, he said he was sure he could get on Apollo 17. Since I haven't heard anything to the contrary I am certain he did. He had arranged it all with Gene Cernan."

"You mean Uncle Herman went to the moon?" Witherspoon asked, his beady little eyes wide open. For once he was impressed.

"He may be up there right now," Aunt Myrtle said. "I often look up at that beautiful moon on a nice balmy night and feel that Herman is looking down at me."

"If he's on the moon he's frozen stiff," Witherspoon said. "Or baked. And how would he breathe with no air up there?"

"Don't ask me," Aunt Myrtle said haughtily. "I'm not a space expert. Perhaps he came back with Apollo 17 but wasn't rescued by helicopter the way the astronauts were. If he had to swim back from some place way out in the ocean, it would take a long time. But I have a feeling that he stayed on the moon. I read some place that there will be no more trips to the moon this century. However, the next century is less than thirty years away and that is no time at all to a turtle. Herman was very resourceful and if he stayed he probably figured out some way to survive."

We were all quiet for several minutes. Witherspoon and I watched while a big tear formed in one of Aunt Myrtle's eyes and fell onto a blade of grass. "If Herman stayed on the moon he may be dead as you say," she said. "I prefer to think otherwise. But in any case he will still be the most famous turtle in the world. Someday someone will go up there and find him or his shell. Think what a time the scientists will have explaining that!"

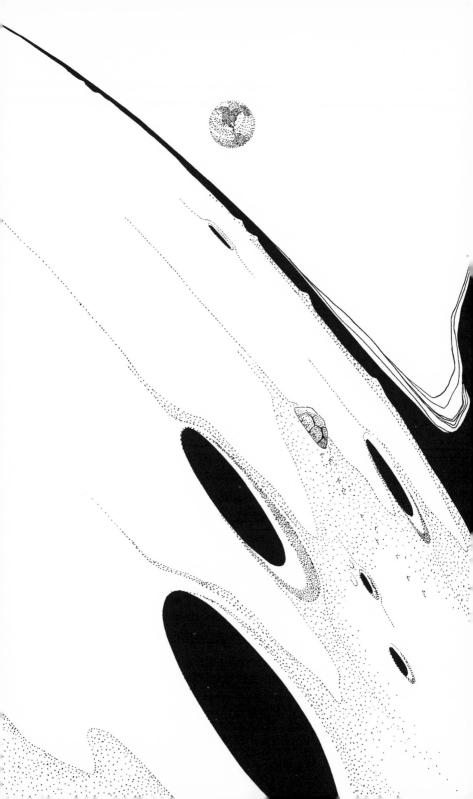

About the Author

KEITH ROBERTSON was born in Iowa and grew up on farms and in small towns in the Midwest. His family moved a great deal, and at one time or another they lived in Kansas, Oklahoma, Minnesota, Wisconsin, and Missouri. After graduation from high school, he served for two years in the Navy and then entered the United States Naval Academy at Annapolis.

When World War II began, Mr. Robertson went into the Navy as a reserve officer and served for five years on a destroyer, in both the Atlantic and the Pacific.

Mr. Robertson has written many popular books for young people, including *The Money Machine* and *Year of the Jeep*. He is probably best known as the creator of the irrepressible Henry Reed. Two of these books, *Henry Reed, Inc.*, and *Henry Reed's Baby-Sitting Service*, have won the William Allen White Children's Book Award. His most recent book was *In Search of a Sandhill Crane*.

Mr. Robertson and his wife live on a small farm in central New Jersey.

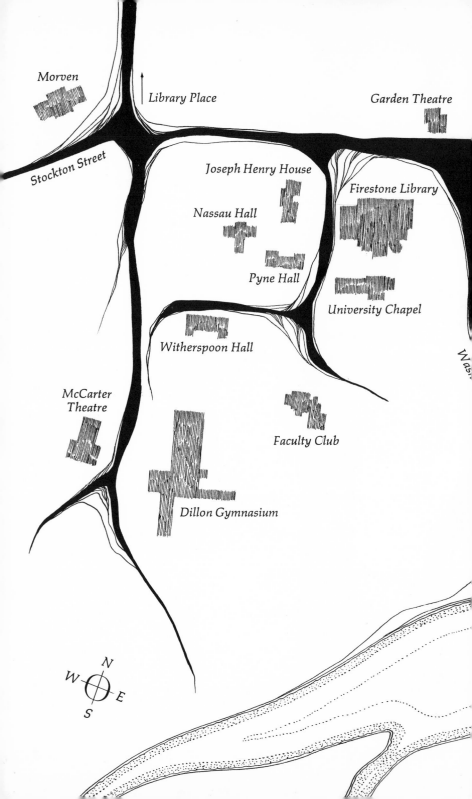

Morven

Library Place

Garden Theatre

Stockton Street

Joseph Henry House

Firestone Library

Nassau Hall

Pyne Hall

University Chapel

Witherspoon Hall

McCarter
Theatre

Faculty Club

Dillon Gymnasium

Wash

N
W E
S